Surrender Language

SURRENDER LANGUAGE

A Novel By

NINA WILSON

Adelaide Books
New York/ Lisbon

2017

SURRENDER LANGUAGE
A Novel
By Nina Wilson

Copyright © 2017 By Nina Wilson

Published by Adelaide Books, New York / Lisbon
An imprint of the Istina Group DBA
adelaidebooks.org

Editor-in-Chief
Stevan V. Nikolic

For any information, please address Adelaide Books
at info@adelaidebooks.org

ISBN13: 978-0-9995164-5-4
ISBN10: 0-9995164-5-0

Printed in the United States of America

To Gordon

Chapter One

"My name is not Mr. Dude. It is not Prof Dude, glasses guy, or even Neal. It is Dr. Neal Basilla. I am not your buddy. My job is not to listen to how accurate you think the movie *Platoon* or *Hanoi Hilton* is," Which always seemed to happen once the word 'Vietnam' or 'vet' came up, especially at the same time and referring to me. "Nor to hear you talk about Captain America as your favorite historical figure. My job is to teach and advise and make your damn brains actually do something resembling thought because apparently schools don't teach people how to think anymore, not that I've seen at least. This is an upper level historical research course hence the 700 in the title. I don't plan to be dealing with freshmen like behavior. I will not tolerate laziness. A hangover is not an excuse to miss an assignment. Your boyfriend breaking up with you and the subsequent binge of ice cream and Netflix is also not an excuse."

Currently I was standing before a class of juniors and seniors at Hunting's Bridge College, most of whom were returning my gaze, blankly, glassily, and for the most part-dumbly. Some were yawning, some were blinking, most just looked like their brains had melted into mush. There was an occasional chuckle giving me the impression that at least one person was listening.

Of course, I was saying one thing and thinking another: 'I am that bastard of a professor who has been here for forty years who expects for you to do the work assigned to you, professionally; I actually expect in-depth discussion: thought. Is thought too much to ask for? Effort?

These kids came to school with brand new cars supplied by their Mommy and Daddy, as well as futons, fridges, and far bigger screens on their TVs than anyone would possibly need. Then they just waltzed around like they owned the place. It wasn't reasonable confidence these kids expressed, it was arrogant and annoying. They felt entitled to everything. They probably wouldn't have to work their way through college like I had. They probably hadn't worked a good hard day in their life at all.

This was my favorite class room, though. Always taught a class here every semester for the past forty years. It had raised seating of three levels with a single straight table in front of the attached seats. The massive windows in the back of the room were serious pains in the ass when I needed to get the curtains down to use the projector especially in this instance when I was trying to be serious. I stood at the head of the classroom with a brand new white board behind me, old lesson plans in my hands, and very smart kids in front of me. Most expected to get A's, and graduate with honors because they knew nothing less. A's were average, B's were below average, didn't I know that? I of all people had to give into their expectations. If only I could laugh out loud at my own joke.

Instead, though, during the second week of class I proceeded to hand out the first quizzes of the semester, already graded in nice, beautiful and bright red pen. Most of these kids had received a B on the quiz. It filled me with joy. Cynical, possibly unnatural joy, but joy nonetheless. It was not out of spite I put B's on most of the papers, but I surely didn't give out A's, they had to be earned, and only one A had been earned.

As I watched the kid's faces as they saw B's and a few lines of red on their pieces of paper, a chorus of questions filled my ears. I only responded, "If you didn't give me insight, only regurgitating facts, you get a B. If you cannot even regurgitate facts, you get a C. The hand out clearly states that I wanted to see detailed insight on how to properly analyze sources." My voice was calm. Most of the students dug out the pale-yellow handout from their folders, read it, and left looking heavier than when they came in 45 minutes ago.

The last person remaining in the room was Denny Helling. He was a good student of mine, well, as far as I could guess from the first two weeks of class. He was idly pushing his chair back and forth with his foot while reading the red markings on his quiz. He was the only student to receive an A. This kid was an odd-looking fellow, and as far as I was aware he was in the theater department's production of *Hamlet.* Because of the play, he seemingly let himself go- his hair had grown into a small bushy, often oily, pony tail at the back of his head, and he usually walked around looking exhausted in clothes that were old and clearly not laundered recently. Although usually frumpy looking, at least he wasn't as distracting as some of his other counterparts who existed in a whirlwind of short shorts and halter tops I expected to come soon when spring finally showed is cowardice self.

Denny stood up from his squeaking seat and said, "Thanks Dr. Neal." There was a small smile on his face that dissipated as soon as he passed the threshold into the hallway.

Finally alone, I packed up my manila folders and walked to my office. I usually left the door ajar, propped open by a mini gargoyle. It was real stone, also a real pain in the ass to move in and out of the building at the beginning and end of the school year. The thing looked rather disturbing, but I liked it. It had the head of a dragon, body of a lion and the wings of a raven. It was a gift from my wife for our twentieth wedding anniversary, thirty-one years ago.

The most wonderful part of my office was the fact it was filled with books: *The Poetic Edda, Asser's Life of King Alfred, The Corolla Sancti Eadmundi,* a full color copy of *The Gospel of Lindisfarne,* Saxo Grammaticus' *History of the Danes,* the *Saga of Ragnars Sons, The Hammer and the Cross,* and *The Annals of Ulster.* I didn't like to use the internet. I was old fashioned. Well, I was old. In my lifetime I had probably read thousands of books, many of which couldn't fit here and cluttered up the space underneath my bed back at home. I couldn't get to them anymore. That would require the ability to bend down. Here, though, at least I had a metal bookshelf installed in the hall, so students could borrow from me. Books were better off being read and used rather than just taking on layers of dust. Of course, most of today's youth preferred the internet, despite my constant request for them to use print sources; the internet just couldn't be trusted. I just stuck with using my email, and the Weather Channel's website, which was better than waiting for the Local on the 8's.

The bookshelf in front of my desk was organized by type. Fist were primary sources, then secondary, and then reference books. I had three sets of Oxford English Dictionaries, one from when I was a very young man, I had received it at the age of fifteen, and one I received when I was forty and one that I bought five years ago. Already I had a feeling that a new dictionary was necessary. Next to the dictionaries were their thesaurus counterparts. Personally, it was interesting to see how language changed just in the time I'd been alive. Beside the thesauruses were binders with my lesson plans from every class I ever taught. Above were all of the textbooks that I ever used in my classes as well as required reading materials, a few of each just so that kids could use them if they forgot theirs. I only taught two sections HIS 750 Topics in Historical Research this semester and there were few required readings, past Kate Turabian's *Manual for Writers*, but I always had kids come to me from other classes. I even had file drawers filled with assignments from every single class that I had taught and some of my favorite papers students had written. I wasn't exactly sure what I was saving these for, but it kept reminding me that there were brains in these kids, they just had to be accessed and used.

I packed up my things, it was time to go home for the day. I had one leather bag, older than any of my students, even the non-traditional ones or, as my students from the UK called them, 'mature'. The bag was a faithful companion, perfectly built to carry all of my papers and it had never broken on me. I shoved the folders into the bag, my hands shaking badly after a long day. It was becoming difficult to pull the zipper shut as I used to, but I managed it. I went down the stairs, holding onto the old wooden railing, feeling all the dents in the wood as I stepped, one slow step at a time. I could hear someone coming from behind me. "Hello Dr. Rogers." I stated once I recognized the shoes. Old green stained trainers, tennis shoes, whatever they were called.

"Still taking the stairs ay?" he asked as I stepped onto the tile landing. There was a large picture window behind me that I couldn't see out of since it was covered completely in a thick ivy, it would have been a better option to avert my eyes.

"Yes." I replied, and I put both hands on the handle of my briefcase. He smiled and touched his light, greying hair before proceeding on, quickly disappearing into the miniature post office housed within Poplar Hall.

I didn't want to go home just yet though… I liked being at the school as much as possible, but the dogs at home needed to go outside and get some exercise. It was selfish of me to stay longer. I hated walking through the door to my home. It was too familiar, and it was too quiet. When I did come home I proceeded on with my normal routine. I opened the door, put my briefcase down, hung my jacket on the hook, and placed my hat on top of that and yelled, "I'm home!" I picked the briefcase up and waited for a response. All I got was my two Australian shepherds running up to greet me. Not Tess. I kept telling myself that she had been dead for over a year, I should have been used to the silence. She used to yell back, "Alright honey!" Instead I got the two excitable dogs; Titan was the oldest, he was sixteen now and a beautiful old blue merle. His best friend Racer had far more energy, almost hitting the wooden railing beside me because he lacked traction on the slick wooden floor. If he wasn't careful, that tail of his would knock me down. I proceeded to put my stuff away before letting them out into the massive backyard to play and run some steam off.

Not even my son was here. Although that death should have been accepted too, he died in the Gulf War over twenty-five years ago. My only son. He wanted to join the military like his father had… he thought it would make me proud, but it killed him too. He was so blown to bits that I didn't even get to see him when they packed him up in a box and sent him home. Tess just had him cremated immediately; she couldn't stand to think of her boy like that. She was better than I at moving past his death. She found ways to cope. She volunteered, everywhere. She helped at the food bank, the homeless shelter, the church she attended, and the city animal shelter. The same shelter she got the two dogs at actually. She always grew up with Australian shepherds on her parent's farm and had wanted them since we got married in '67. It wasn't so easy for me. Nothing was as easy for me as it was for her.

Everything in the house changed when Tess got ill, though. We brought in a hospital bed and put it in the living room. The damn thing took up a great deal of space and everything had been moved around. I sold the love-seat and one of the couches while she was sick to help pay for everything since Tess told me not to dip into the saving's account. So now there was only a small couch and my arm chair, the beat-up old coffee table that I was forbidden to sell, and the small table that was next to my arm chair. That table was over a hundred years old and clearly just as beaten up but very dear to my heart.

I took down most of the family photos after she died. I couldn't stand to look at them. Now they were safely hidden inside the coffee table's little compartment. Once I considered duct taping the doors closed. Or getting a lock. Thus, the walls were mostly bare, which wasn't a good thing either. The emptiness made the already large house, larger.

I sold the big dining room table, we never used it after Benjamin was killed anyways. Instead there was just a smaller table in the kitchen that we used to eat at. And it still stayed pristine as if someone was going to use it today. I felt guilty taking away the things Tess had cherished, but I couldn't stand to have them around. The many cookbooks she gathered over the years had been donated, her collection of glass chickens that had lined the top shelves of the kitchen were given to the church that she was a part of for a rummage sale. Her sewing room was emptied and all of those things were also given to her church to be used by the quilting club. Now it was a storage room. I didn't go in there unless I really had to.

Tess always loved to decorate the house for holidays, any holiday. If it was celebrated by the English or by Americans, then we decorated for it. I didn't do that now. In the storage room was all of our Christmas decorations, and fall decorations, Halloween, Easter, everything, but I couldn't even look at them, especially not the Christmas ones. Just last Christmas I didn't see the purpose in putting them up. It was always Tess's thing. It brought her such joy, but I missed her too much and it seemed almost hypocritical to put them up with the assumption that I was going to celebrate with people. The only thing that I had planned for any holidays were things at the school. I didn't have anyone to celebrate with or give gifts to. Tess was the friend-maker, she dragged me all over creation to her holiday parties with her church lady friends. Last Christmas they never returned my calls, or my obligatory Christmas cards.

It was still hard for me to fathom that she was dead. I forgot to think while she was sick. I didn't want to process and file away what was happening into my memory. I didn't want to remember her that way. It was the worst feeling to know that she was going to die, to be able to smell it, to see her deteriorate to the point where I had to carry her into the bathroom, bathe her, dress her, brush her teeth because she was unable to do it herself. I hated that I could carry her. I had Parkinson's already, although she didn't know anymore, her mind had become partially delusional from the illness and medication. She was so small that it didn't matter. That disease, that cancer, made her into a sack of bones. She shrunk to half her size in just a few months, all of her clothes were loose on her, but it didn't matter, she was stuck in a hospital gown while at home regardless.

I hated night the worst. I would keep the radio on until the last minute or play records and CD's of Gregorian chants and most of the time I would delve into my research, fill my brain with facts and dates instead of anything else. I had a lecture presentation coming up on the historical significance of the island of Lindisfarne, before and after it had been sacked by piratical Scandinavians in 793. I was perfecting my paper. I liked to remind myself that a body of work is never completed, it can always be improved upon. It was useful that way.

Research really was the heart and soul of history. Realizing connections and looking deep into the reality of the past was extraordinary. It was something taken for granted. My students in Topics of Historical Research, my favorite class to teach, were to compile a reasonable body of work by the end of the semester and it was supposed to be their responsibility. Being an upper level course, I wasn't going to lead them along like little puppies. If they were to succeed in the field of study they had chosen, they needed to learn to do it themselves, and only come for questions on their own volition, not mine. Not one student had even brought the research paper up until Monday of the fourth week of class, and yet I was excited to see what ideas these young people would come up with.

It was February now. The worst month that ever existed. I hated that the cold still was around. I hated that the snow was still on the ground and had gone grey. I hated that I hadn't seen the sunlight directly in over three months. I hated that there was Valentine's Day and I had to pretend like it was alright that my wife couldn't be there with me. My wife who I had been married to for fifty-one years.

Yet I had to get over it, just like I had to get over so many other things, and learn that I wasn't going to last very long anyway. The college already recognized that fact. In August I received, in the mail, not by the grace of someone's face and mouth, a warning that within the year my class load would become reduced drastically and come May, I'd retire. No amount of face to face complaining and rejecting of the mail had done anything. I deserved to have a longer warning as I had tenure. I deserved to work at HBC. It was as if they had no respect for wisdom. As if age was a disability in and of itself. Yet I realized that I'd be pressed to retire against my will. They wouldn't stop. They knew what they wanted.

Chapter Two

I was sitting comfortably in my office. The old chair had been in my possession probably a good forty years, bought originally from a Sears and Roebuck catalog. It had gorgeous tearing black leather and bumpy wheels. It had even survived a raging fire which had ravished half of Poplar Hall in the mid-nineties.

I looked outside of the window, peering past a photo of Tess standing on the land bridge to the Holy Island of Lindisfarne. It was gray outside and the wind was rushing past her. She was standing before the golden dunes that covered a majority of the island's wildlife sanctuary. Tess had just cut her hair short because it was beginning to gray. With the wind, her hair partially covered her freckled, wrinkling face. Her burly, crisp, blue-green parka was remaining evidence of the early nineties styles. Even though we had just lost Benjamin at that time there was still that smile on her face and all that light in her eyes.

There was a horrible, dense misty fog hanging over the open clearing in the center of the school. The lamps were on even though it was the morning. Those lights did very little except for making the fog yellow rather than a dingy grey. I touched the folder in front of me containing a print copy of my final version of my article. I worked on the research on the Holy Island of Lindisfarne and the Community of St. Cuthbert for over twelve years. The island was the place of origin of the literary craft in the British Isles, as well as one of the centers for the creation of illuminated manuscripts. Even after the monks were chased from the island by Vikings, they spread throughout Europe to teach the craft. It was a brilliant place. Just a few days ago I received word that my work was going to be published, which was nice. For a moment, I just stared at it, feeling slightly odd that it was finished. It wasn't as if it was my life's work. I didn't have work that had taken my entire life to complete, but it had taken up so many years nonetheless.

Denny came to my office that morning while I was looking at the final article. He quietly knocked on the white door frame, and appeared rather nervous and shy, standing with his hands firmly in the pockets of his gray zip-up hoodie, and his knees tight together. "Hello, come in." I said. I was trying to sound friendly, but I never really knew what my voice sounded like to other people. Students here seemed to speak a foreign language to me.

"Hi, I was wondering if we could talk about the paper." he began. His voice, clouded by an English accent, sounded oddly proper, like he belonged on BBC. My wife, who was also from England had a voice of someone who was not trained to sound British, but she was from a rural village called Alnwick in Northumberland.

"Yes, come in, come in. Do you have any topic ideas?" I asked, crossing my arms and leaning back in my chair.

"Very loosely. I really like France. I've been learning French since third grade and thought I could do something like that." I wanted to laugh, honestly.

"The French?" I smiled and took in a deep breath. "What period are you thinking?"

"The French Revolution, maybe." he said, his eyes flickered around the room.

"I did note that when you do a paper, you must make a contribution to the field in some manner. Many people in the past have written about the French Revolution. Do you think that you could come up with a solid theory? Something new?" I asked.

He rubbed his hands together, still avoiding eye contact for the most part and simply shrugged. "I can look and see if I can. There are other interesting things I've been thinking of… like the Battle of Verdun. I heard that Tolkien, the guy who wrote *Lord of the Rings*, based Gandalf saying 'you shall not pass' to the Balrog, off of the battle of Verdun. It was their saying against the Germans in World War I or something like that."

"One of the only times they didn't surrender." I replied, sneaking in my disdain for the French.
His face twisted into a smile and he said, "Do I speak surrender language then since I can speak French?"

"Do you?" I asked. He nodded. "Then yes, you speak surrender language. You know the history, it's not a world war until France surrenders."

"Oh, is that so?"

"Even in the Hundred Year's War after Charlemagne, things kind of just fell apart for the French."

"All the way back there in time? It wasn't even France yet, was it?" he asked, crossing his arms, brow furrowing curiously. He was becoming increasingly comfortable. His shoulders weren't so close to his ears now; they were starting to slump the way they were supposed to.

"It was Francia at that time, close enough, and Charlemagne, poor man, after everything he ever worked for was taken from Francia... he was working so hard on literacy, currency, getting what would eventually become France, out of the Dark Ages."

"And what happened?" he asked.

"The Scandinavians came in and destroyed it."

"Isn't that all they do?" he asked, smiling.

"Ah be careful on your assumptions, Denny. Well, to expand upon that, it was more along the lines of he had lots of sons... and he liked them all I guess, and so he separated his empire into pieces for them to control. So after he worked so hard to unify the land, he tore them apart again, and once he was gone... well, his sons started to quarrel amongst themselves and they never managed to get their feet on the ground again, I guess. But about those Scandinavians... they are far more than piracy and pillaging." I was still smiling. I hadn't smiled this much in a while. "Taking over England, forcing Alfred the Great to conglomerate all of that into one country rather than the four it was- once of course, they had been kicked out. They also took over Ireland, and made it into a strong economic power while they were there. They helped in the destruction of the Picts, paving the way for the lovely Scots to come in from Ireland and make what once was Pictland into what is now Scotland. They initiated trade with the Islamic world…" I sighed. "It's not just all that pillaging and plundering, although to get to that point they did pillage and plunder." It always came back to that, but that was the field of study I was in, it had to be expected. "Have you seen that bookshelf in the hallway?"

"It's hard to miss Dr. Neal, it's massive."

"On there, there are a few books to get you started on the French Revolution. Their bibliographies are great and should get you some sources, so you can see how far along you can get in this project, or if you really want to do the battle of Verdun, there is a book on France's contribution to World War I, as well as any book by Tolkien should be out there. You could look into evidence of world war themes throughout the books."

"Thanks Dr. Neal!" he said and searched for the books. That kid had some potential.

"Just remember for your subject: narrow, narrow, narrow!" I couldn't say that enough. I really couldn't.

A week later, I was walking hurriedly outside to get to my office in time for another meeting with Denny. He emailed me saying he was having some troubles figuring out what he wanted to do for his paper still. Many of my students were having the same issues and that was to be expected. Yet most of them were just dabbling in ideas. At the moment only Denny showed that he was putting real effort into making some progress. Normally there would be people coming in and asking me about sources, what was primary, what was secondary, how to make a good outline, how to cite... I saw very little of that from any of my students this semester and it was concerning. How much prodding did they need? I didn't have some electrified cattle sticks to poke them with. I could invest in one. Without fail, year after year they were getting worse at doing things themselves. All of these students, being juniors and seniors already had an introductory research class and its purpose was to teach them how to do research, but in that case they were led along step by step. This class was their test, to see if they could do it on their own and they were expected to do so. If they were to fail, it wasn't by me; I was merely an advisor ready and available to help when students needed it. They could complain all they wanted on course evaluations, the dean of faculty knew well enough what was expected out of them. Tenure was already there. It wasn't my senility getting in the way. I was fully functional. Fully. Functional.

Recently, though I was getting behind when it came to getting from place to place. Driving was becoming an issue; my hands wouldn't stay still long enough for me to drive the two miles from my house to school in an efficient manner. It was too cold out to walk just yet, and I wasn't going to risk angering my muscles, they were already causing me enough trouble. So, I drove 20 miles per hour. Five below the speed limit. That's how slow Tess drove. She always thought the limit meant you couldn't go above, how adorable. I couldn't laugh at her anymore.

I held the folders in my gloved hands as I walked along

the crooked sidewalk from the parking lot. I hadn't any room in the leather bag hanging from my shoulder. There was ice on the ground and I was trying to be careful. The last thing I needed was to take a tumble. My hands were trembling so badly. I focused all my energy into holding onto the folders, and yet it was no use. The trembling was not something I could control. I became distracted from the ridiculously breathtaking cold that was blasting in my face, making it feel like my skin would shatter and cover the ground… and all the papers went careening onto the wet, icy cement, some carried away by the damned wind. I tried to pick up what I could, and only ended up dumping more onto the ground.

"Dr. Neal!" Denny was running over to me, his back-pack bouncing on his black button-up coat. "Let me get that, let me get that!" he said, a little out of breath. He put the two cups of coffee on the ground and ran after what I had dropped. I picked up the coffee, trying to be helpful, thankfully they had lids. He laughed and put all the papers into his bag and we walked into Poplar Hall. We got to my office and I put the two cups down and he handed me the papers from his bag. "There we go." he stated casually. I looked them over, some had soaked straight through, others were fortunate enough to only touch the extremely dry snow, and the wind blasted whatever precipitation could have wetted them right off.

While I situated my things, Denny looked around the room and his eyes landed on an old photo hanging on my wall.

"Where is that from?" he asked. The picture was of myself and some of my buddies.

"I was in Vietnam." I said. "At eighteen years old. I'm the one in the middle. The two to my right were brothers," I stood up and took the picture down. "That's Big Jim, a Navajo." I pointed to a relatively massive but scrawny young man standing with a bandana wrapped around his head. "And that's Bo. He was from New Orleans." I smiled. It was not a happy smile.

"You were in Vietnam? Does anyone know that here?" he asked curiously. He studied the photo like it was gold. It was far from gold, in fact it was written up on the back to pieces, torn, had water stains. I carried it around in my pocket and wallet so long that it had been sufficiently abused.

"I don't think so, besides the chair of the department." I said. "She kept asking if I would teach a class on it, but I kept turning her down saying that it wasn't my field of study. Firsthand accounts aren't degrees. Plus, it would be odd to teach a class on something I experienced so vividly myself." I paused. "No one wants to remember this war, or even admit that it happened."

"That is one way of putting it." he stated. "So I...I'm having trouble with this paper. I know it hasn't been that long, but I figure that if I want to tackle something like this, I should start early."

"That is a good mindset to have Denny." Thank God he wasn't an idiot. "I mentioned in class that you need to pick a topic that is important to you, good things come from people who care. Why is this important to you?"

He shrugged, and looked behind him, and then up to the ceiling and off to the side before finally saying, "I don't know, uh, my sister, Bridget, she made me take French

classes with her throughout our time in boarding school."
Boarding school? My God, my God, what parents would do
that to their child? He smiled sadly and shook his head,
"She'd read all these books about French history because she
thought it was so glamorous, and glittery, or something like
that. She said that she wished her life could be that way. We
grew up studying English history, but it seems just like a
bunch of guts and war. The kings look like they belong in a
dump rather than on the front page of Vogue. She marveled
at their attire, their hair, the life they lived and how they
were so focused on culture. She loved how they took
initiative in the French Revolution even if they couldn't
make their minds up after it happened. I suppose she just
instilled all those thoughts in me."

I nodded and said, "And your interest in World War I?"

"It's easier to access." He laughed.

"If that's the only reason, then don't do it." I replied.
"Now don't be like the French, learn to make decisions."

He shook his head and said, "You really have issues
with the French don't you?" he was chuckling lightly and
rubbing his hand on his arm. He did that a lot.

"Of course. The English and French are known for
their disagreements."

"But you're American." he replied.

"My wife wasn't. She was English." But the French
were the ones that got me into Vietnam.

"If you really want to know why I want to write this
paper… my sister's sick right now and it's hard to talk to
her. I wanted something that we could talk about." His eyes
looked up at me and made eye contact.

I replied, "Distractions are nice. The sooner you get to work; the sooner you can talk to her about this. Alright? There are plenty of sources out there, you just have to find the right ones and learn to use them. If you have any questions I'm here, or there's email."

"Thanks, Dr. Neal. I hope your papers didn't get too harmed by the ice."

"They'll live." I said. He left, digging his hands deep into the pockets of his coat and walked with his head down. Truthfully, I wasn't alright with my hands letting me drop such important documents. It was a good thing that none of them were the student's papers, but they were my own notes. I was a man who liked to handwrite as much as possible. I felt that handwriting helped solidify the thoughts in my mind. Although increasingly my own writing was getting difficult to read. From the perfect script I worked for my entire life there now was this rough chicken scratch. But I hated technology because of the control that I'd have to exert on my hands to type something with any speed was enormous, and even with the effort, it wouldn't be much better. I hated anything touch screen, it was too sensitive and I wouldn't be able to get anything done. I liked my old phone here that still had buttons, and my home phone had the redial button on it. It wasn't like I had a lot of people to call anyways.

I laid the papers out flat so they could dry and be salvaged. I stared at them wondering if I would ever be able to do research like this again. I spent a great deal of my life writing papers, and giving lectures, that I didn't know what else to do. People always said retirement was wonderful, that you could go golfing daily, spend time with your family, learn to paint. I couldn't do any of that. My body was too stiff to golf (not that I ever liked golf to begin with), I had no family left, and I couldn't possibly learn to paint; my hands wouldn't allow it. There was nothing. I supposed I could read books into oblivion but that would require me to be able to handle them, and mange to turn the pages.

I begged the college to let me stay, but they only responded that my disease was too big of a distraction to learning and inhibited my ability to be a proper teacher. Being the stubborn man I was, I wanted to sue since I had tenure, but I knew that they were right. Soon I wouldn't be able to stand very well, I was already beginning to hunch over despite my constant attempts to stand straight, sit straight and even lay straight. I was doing my best, but Parkinson's wasn't going away. According to the doctor, he couldn't cure it even with all the fancy medication that he kept prescribing me so I wouldn't shoot myself.

Chapter Three

I sat at my desk. As if ready for a fight, I had a bottle of water and handkerchief. In front of me was my notebook. My handwriting was getting so small like chicken scratch, but I supposed that my walking was doing the same thing. When I was younger I was a runner, I loved the feeling of quasi-flight. Currently I couldn't even imagine walking more than two miles an hour. I had to shuffle my way across life. Once I found myself at the tops of trees, or having got in trouble for swimming in nearby farm ponds. Now I could hardly stand up from a chair now without the assistance of the table in front of me, or without getting dizzy. That dictionary on the top shelf probably would never be used again since I couldn't reach it. I was a pathetic mess. Age was a cruel, cruel thing I realized. I had seen it be kind to no one, but I guess that wasn't Time's job description, it was giving its attention to the young at the moment.

I was glad that Tess wasn't here to see me like this. I was diagnosed close to a decade and a half ago, but it really didn't get that bad until Tess got sick. I hid as much of the trouble Parkinson's caused me as possible while she was alive. I didn't want to burden her with anything. Through the illnesses I supposed we could experience the same things together, but I didn't have to be pricked with needles constantly or go through radiation. I lost my hair far before I got sick, so I didn't have to worry about that. Yet I thought she lost her hair with grace because she decided to shave it all off and then she knitted her own hats with flowers and bows and beautiful designs. She thought of it as an opportunity for growth in her crafting. She always saw every experience as an opportunity for growth...

But selfish me wished that she was here to help. It was awfully hard getting around. I was beginning to wish that I could have one of my dogs with me at all times. I could normally get my hands to work better after petting one of them. I could also walk easier because they would help my balance. One of the dogs was always next to me in the morning so I could lean on them to get out of bed. Tess loved dogs and trained all of them like they belonged in a circus. She thought it was fun, and when she was younger, she wanted to train dogs to be service animals. She had to give up on that dream because reality got in the way, but nonetheless, she trained ours. The dogs knew how to open cupboards and doors, and the fridge. They could help me get things so I could sit in my nice, comfy arm chair and relax.

The doctors said I needed to do more exercise and whenever it was nice outside, I would walk to Hunting's Bridge. It took about an hour, but I usually took a dog with me. Titan was my old buddy; he knew the path well. He was having issues with stairs as much as I was. Racer was the biggest and the strongest still and I would take him with me sometimes. Despite his name, Racer was more patient

I was with myself. He didn't mind going really slow. This way he had the ability to sniff everything in sight, and pee on at least half of it. Then whichever of the two came with me would live in my office for the day and people would come by and say hi, bring them their leftover food and there would be some pigging out, plenty of walks, a few games of fetch... All was well.

Hunting's Bridge College, a good ten years ago or so, complained that I was bringing my dog to work, but I affirmed the fact that no student here had an issue with it. I had Titan then, and he didn't leave my office without me or a student I trusted for a short walk. I kept a gate in the doorway so he could see out and students could come and visit. He did not disturb the faculty. None of my dogs ever barked while at school, they knew better. They were supposed to make people feel more comfortable with their environment. Was that too much to ask? If simply petting an animal could help students get their work done and not feel like they had to drink themselves into oblivion every weekend, then it was useful.

Kids here weren't used to struggling with anything but their sexuality, some money issues, and their constant boredom and lack of attention span until college hit. Things changed. Stress was debilitating at times. Dogs were helpful in that matter.

Although recently I noticed that every five seconds some students would look at their phone to check text messages, email, Facebook, that thing with the bird, whatever it was, so clearly those things were more important to them than the class or my existence for that matter. I realized after forty years of teaching that history can be exhaustingly boring at times. If not dry as a bone, and dense as a brick. We didn't get to dissect cats, rant about politicians that often, or blow things up. My beginning of the semester speech normally dealt with: you are where you are because of the past, and so on and so forth. That didn't seem to matter because of the massive amounts of writing, reading and critical thinking that had to be put into the class anyway. I couldn't make it shiny and pretty, and films could only do so much to help. Films, in fact, made me cringe. Of course it was bringing history to life, but it wasn't doing it in a way that I could describe as being historically accurate instead of fictional. I let it slip once that I was in Vietnam and next thing I knew my class was filled with a chorus 'what did you thinking about Platoon?' What was I supposed to say 'the heart beat in the back of the soundtrack practically killed me'? 'It was worse than that'? 'I never met anyone who looked like Johnny Depp?'

I had announced to my history class I was doing my final presentation tonight in the auditorium and that it would concern Lindisfarne. Being the smart kids, they were, a few individuals had been asking me questions about the project to change the topic of discussion in class. They knew the topic as I used my own research as a way to describe the process of searching for sources, how to analyze them, what to look for, and how to cite. Still I doubted they would come. It was a Monday night, and they probably had something more important to do like watching TV and killing their brain cells.

Nonetheless, the lecture important to me. I figured that this was the last presentation I was ever going to do, at least at HBC, and so I wanted to look nice. I wore my favorite sweater, a faded navy blue cable-knit, and a tan sport coat with a matching bowtie. I knew I looked like a geek, according to the kids, but I didn't care. I felt comfortable wearing this, and I looked quite dapper in the mirror.

When I arrived to the auditorium, a bit later than I originally intended to, I saw that a reception was being set up outside the seating area, including tea, coffee, water, and sugar cookies. As long as I had been married to a Brit, I still couldn't down tea. It was still just hot leaf juice to me and that made me feel like nothing more than a sophisticated rabbit.

Most of the people in attendance meandering about in the auditorium lobby were faculty and staff. I recognized Katja immediately. She was one of the youngest people here, and her bright smile was almost jarring and stood out amongst the others. The banana yellow cardigan she was wearing didn't help, and neither did the equaly yellow shoes. She exuded sunshine. Dean Carlton was here as well, the man who saw me accidently stumble down the stairs a few months ago, walking by saying, "I guess I'm going to need to talk to you about that sickness of yours one of these days, Neal." He managed to shove me into producing this lecture earlier in the semester than I intended. Last year I was hoping to get a glimpse into the annual Good Friday pilgrimage to the Holy Island to share with the school, but I wasn't going to get a chance. I had to make do with the subject of my actual article instead. He was smiling, happily talking to a few colleagues. Avoiding people as much as possible, I checked to make sure that the projector was up. I had visual aids because that was what people these days needed, even the professors around me currently.

The audience began filing in, sitting down in the old blue velvet seating. The color was just a tad lighter than the navy of my sweater, and probably much older. This auditorium in the Gregory Blau Arts Center was the smaller of the two in HBC, and because of that, thankfully I didn't need to use a microphone. The white material hung on the walls was meant to help sound travel without echoing, at least that's what Carlton told me. The clicker for the projector was going to be a challenge enough. Maybe it was my nerves, but my hands were worse than they had been in weeks. I kept assuring myself that I'd be fine. I practiced this many times over and I knew this history like the back of my hand and in fact I'd been to the island a dozen times. My wife and I went there to visit about ten times while she was alive, and I had been there twice since. It was a place we always found very special between us. If people cared enough, I'd like to share it- hence me standing here in front of room of people who probably felt obligated to be here.

I sat down in the front row until I was introduced by Dean Carlton. I was called an honored professor, a good friend, so on and so forth. If I was so awesome, why the hell were they making me retire before I wanted to? It wasn't going to be retirement; it was going to be my death. Bitterness aside I couldn't let the nerves and anger get to me because it would make me all worked up and then my hands would tremor more than they already were. Pockets weren't working to hide them; the flaps of my jacket just shook like I was in a tornado. I tried sitting on them for a moment, but it only made them hurt and cramp slightly and they were still going to shake regardless. There was nothing I could do. It was like a pervading feeling of helplessness, losing control of one's body was cruel.

I stood up and did a brief introduction on my topic before beginning the power point presentation. As I was speaking, the door at the back of the small auditorium opened, letting in a flood of golden late afternoon light. Denny snuck in, attempting to be quiet. He wore his black jacket with stage makeup on his face, making him look gaunt and hollow. The rings around his eyes made him look like he was in worse shape than I was. I made eye contact with him and he came and sat in the front row.

"Lindisfarne had created a very influential church by the six hundreds. They held huge lands, extensive grants from the Northumbrian royal house, and furthered Northumbrian royal interests by functioning as centers of governments before the destruction of the monastery, firstly, in 793. The history of Northumbria, even, has been divided and splintered, the only central history to follow cleanly within Northumbria, is that of the Holy Island itself."

I had some issues hitting the right button on the clicker. I just had some issues holding the damn thing too; well I just issues in general. Denny reached out his hand and I gave the clicker to him. I looked at him directly whenever I wanted the next slide to come up. I calmed down and proceeded like everything was completely normal.

"After the creation of the Danelaw following the conquering of England by the Great Heathen Army, the remaining successors to the destroyed Northumbrian kingdom was the kingdom of York, and mainly important to my research: the Community of St. Cuthbert which was on the island of Lindisfarne. It had a heavy hand in the politics and policies of Northumbria." I nodded to Denny to switch the slide. "Both assisted the new booming economic market with an influx of agricultural surplus, and wide spread trade that came with the new Danish leaders."

The lecture lasted roughly 45 minutes. Afterwards I answered questions for about ten minutes before the reception in the common area outside of the auditorium. There was a short bombardment of people wanting to shake my hands. Thankfully my hands were very good at shaking. Lastly, Denny exited the auditorium, covering his head with his jacket hood. "Thanks for coming." I said to Denny. Simply, I was grateful for his presence and his help.

"I thought I was going to miss it. I've been practicing dying for the past two hours," he said with a laugh. I was a bit confused, not connecting the get-up to the whole dying thing. "Don't worry, it was just poison… well and a sword… first a poisoned sword and then just poison… oh I'm sorry, I'm very tired. I can't… I can't talk well right now. It's all like a blur. I should just stop rambling." He continued to laugh. Shakespeare, I thought, that explains everything.

"So what production are you doing? Hamlet, right?" I asked. Denny was sipping on some tea while I put my hands behind my back, trying to hide them. My legs were getting tired from standing for so long. They began to shake just slightly, making me lose my balance, so I held onto the table behind me for support. I wished I dug out that cane in my closet to use tonight. I just didn't want people seeing me with it. I didn't want them to think I was that far along and that far gone. It was a sign of weakness.

"Yes, Hamlet." Denny said.

"Ah really?"

"And I happen to be Hamlet. We also get to practice the fun of sword fighting. Tomorrow, though, there is a man coming down from the graduate program I applied to, and he is coming to see the first run through of the production. I'm hoping that it will make the scholarship a bit bigger."

He jammed his hands into his pockets and shivered. "Congratulations. So you were accepted?"

"Yes,"

"Good luck to you." I stated. "And thank you again for coming."

Chapter Four

I drove home even though it was dark outside. My eye sight wasn't the greatest in this light, but thankfully I could still manage to drive. My car was old enough that I had to put force behind the steering wheel to make it do what I wanted it to, so it wasn't just going back and forth at my hand's whim. Even as I held the wheel with all my mind focused on keeping my body parts still, my hands still went on shaking like before. It didn't matter how much I focused, they and every other part of my body had a mind of its own.

When I arrived home, the dogs welcomed me. I couldn't even imagine living here if it wasn't for them. It would be too silent. Too dead. However, Titan was walking slowly now; he wasn't as fit as he used to be. I understood, it came with age. Age was cruel. Racer, though, was keeping to his namesake, running around the house like he always did, trying to get Titan to follow him. He was ruthless on the old dog as he wasn't that much fun to play with, but neither was I. I couldn't even throw his ball that far anymore. Getting my arm to raise that high was in the realm of impossibility. I tried though. I tried.

I sat in my easy chair and took out a novel I was reading, *Old Man and the Sea*. I thought now I was older, I could understand Santiago a bit better. The first time I read this as a young man I just thought he was some nut hopelessly in love with a giant fish. Now he was a nut, though, who was facing death. At least I had something in common with him.

I asked Titan to get my water bottle from the fridge. He knew what the words meant and how to do it. That was something Tess taught them to do, it took forever to train him though, he was always so distractible. The poor old guy was getting as bad as I, but if I didn't ask him to do something, he'd be depressed. So, with his tail wagging he went to the fridge, pulled on the rope that was attached to the handle, and opened it. Racer stood so the door didn't open too far, and helped him close it when the bottle was fetched. Both were just so smart and so kind with one another, they almost felt like people. Tess saw dog's as people with souls. I pet the old dog's head and he curled up next to my chair on his bed. Racer ran around, playing with a ball, always full of energy. I wished it was nicer outside, I would let them out all day long, but the cold would cause Titan's joints to freeze up and he didn't need any more of that, and the two didn't like to be separated.

I began to doze off. It was only nine but I figured I deserved to go to bed early. I was very tired. My research was done…I felt oddly empty, lonely, and had that odd, annoying, melancholy feeling stuck in my chest and my throat, burning through my flesh. Yet nothing was actually burning anything. It was all my mind, my tired, hallucinatory mind.

I almost felt like crying but I hadn't cried since Tess died. Before that I hadn't cried since my son died and considering that there hadn't been any deaths recently, I didn't have much reason to cry. I entered my bedroom. The closet was half empty, my wife's clothes weren't there any longer, yet I kept her half of the closet spotless. Her specific hamper, as she always liked that they were separate, was still there: white wicker with a porcelain top painted with pink and yellow roses. It was our son Benjamin's favorite place to hide during hide and seek. I kept one pair of her slippers sitting on her side of the bed, although Titan took up that space by now rather than just sleeping by my feet. Tess's jewelry box was still on the dresser, filled with her jewelry. I went through it occasionally, feeling the familiarity it brought me. Her wedding jewelry was there, although I was never able to find out where the dress went. One wedding photo was kept underneath the bed. We looked so innocent and young in the photo, but I knew my innocence was gone by the time I married Tess. War had a tendency to do that to a man.

I paced for a little while. I always thought pacing would clear my mind, but it always made things worse. I used to go running when I was stressed, but that wasn't happening. I tried using a stationary bike a while back and that wasn't helpful either. I just didn't have enough control over anything and my muscles were just so stiff and sore. My anger caused more stress and that stress was causing tension and that made me even angrier.

I was a pathetic hunk of meat, and uncontrollable meat at that.

Monday rolled around. I didn't want Monday, but I didn't really feel like any other day of the week would be enjoyable either. The weekend was only nice because I began to appreciate not having responsibilities for two days. I just cleaned over the weekend, trying to make my house look acceptable, like I was in perfect condition, like all was well. Life was about pretending, wasn't it? If I could just pretend until it'd become reality, all would truly be well.

I woke up promptly at seven. Racer helped me out of bed, and Titan slowly got up from his place beside me. Both yawned like clockwork and I let them outside once we reached the kitchen where the sliding glass door was. I shuffled to the bathroom and brushed my teeth and combed what hair I had left and took my meds. I was glad that I finally got the fancy caps on my pill bottles so it didn't take twenty minutes and eighty different methods to open the damned things. I poured myself a cup of coffee that brewed overnight. It was more out of habit than need these days. I slept plenty, but the warmth was appreciated. I didn't use my mugs anymore, only the travel cup kind with the lids on them so I could warm my hands and not risk spilling. I then got dressed in some good clothes, wore my favorite thick stockings I received five years ago as a gift. I didn't wear crappy clothes. I got to wear crappy clothes when I was a kid, I worked my ass off enough that I deserved to wear respectable good clothing for the rest of my life, no matter the situation even if I did have to fight the buttons for half the morning. I wasn't going to wear those stupid, shitty, old man pants. I was going to keep wearing my ironed, pleated, dress pants, my sweaters and my button up shirts because that's what I worked for. I worked for respect and dammit I was going to look respectable.

I planned on walking to school that day. The sun was very bright and the snow melted. I figured there wouldn't be a lot of ice left and once again I could pretend like all was back to normal by returning to my normal routine. I called for Racer to come over but Titan did too. "Sorry Titan, you're going to have to stay here." I said to him. My voice sounded unholy breaking the verbal silence that filled my house. I pet his head and kissed his cheek. His tail wagged a bit. We were a pathetic pair.

I put Racer on a leash. Titan didn't need one anymore and hadn't in years, but Racer was still very curious about the things around him and would wander off if I didn't stop him. Once he was safely hooked up, we shuffled forward onto the sidewalk. I focused on myself completely so I could try to actually walk, but it just wasn't going to happen. I hadn't been able to walk in a while. I wondered when it was that I lost control over that simple action. When I was young I could just tell it to do something and it would, to an extent, I wasn't a dancer or anything like that, but I was a Marine. I had to do a lot of shitty physical work, and now I couldn't even walk with dignity. Instead I was the Hunchback of Notre Dame.

I'd been shuffling for an hour when I got to Poplar. We walked through two blocks of student housing, dormitories and apartments when I entered the section of academic buildings. Everything was named after trees:

Aspen, Maple, Cedar, Willow, Locust, Sycamore, Balsam, and Cyprus. Either it meant the one who named them was creative, or dull. I basically lived in the humanities building, though, which was one of the oldest on campus. It was made of a dark, red brick that was getting browner with age and covered in a very similarly dark ivy that climbed up to the top of the curved roof.

Once I reached the front door, I realized that I was beyond the definition of cold, completely frigid. While walking I focused on getting one foot in front of the other and didn't notice. Finally reaching my office, I slumped onto my desk chair before remembering that I had to put up the dog gate for Racer, who seemed impervious to the cold. He had a coat of fur, I didn't. I didn't even have much hair on my head. I had to wear hats because people didn't need to see the shiny top of my head and the liver spots dotting it. I didn't feel like moving at all. I closed my eyes and took a breather. I wished I had a hot cup of coffee.

When time for class came, I still wanted that hot cup of coffee. I hadn't completely defrosted yet. Thankfully I had only two classes this semester, the board thought I should be slowing down. Both classes I taught were research based. Research was my favorite part and often I would find myself immersed into the material, allowing myself to forget my mobility issues, the Parkinson's, everything that hurt. I could feel my hands calming during class as I spoke, and I was able to speak fluently and coherently. I felt intelligent again. I felt useful. There were questions being asked and answered, the students were getting work done. It was an accomplishment to see them on this journey, and to see their brains actually start waking up and getting real intellectual thinking done, working through problems and finding solutions. It was gorgeous. They had already acquired so many skills… but those stupid phones. I wasn't even sure how they could possibly see them in the lighting of the classroom. The window behind them was so bright, it made it impossible to see the projector and I had seen what phones looked like in the sunlight. Yet the students were sneaky and desperate enough that they couldn't disconnect from the internet or their text messaging for one hour. All I asked of their direct attention was one hour, three times a week.

I believed it was time to implement the basket method. I used it many times before, but only in recent years. I would put a basket at the front of the classroom where every student put their phone and then they could pick it up when they left. If a phone was seen being used during class it would live in my office for twenty-four hours, a time period most of the students couldn't fathom living without their technology for.

It was rather entertaining to see them give up their beloved possessions, I almost thought I would see them kissing the phones and saying a formal goodbye. I could see when students tried to sneak phones in, the kids outside the classroom, seeing the basket would hide them in pockets of their backpack. Realizing this, I would watch them closely and once those phones were in sight, they were on the white -board shelf and then in a drawer in my office. Many other professors asked why I was so harsh on phone usage in my class. I could only reply that they had no reason to be chatting with their friends over text message because it sure as hell wasn't about history class. In fact, there were multiple comments that I had seen on student's screens about how ugly, horrible, and annoying I am. For the most part those were taken as compliments because I was doing my job right and not being a pushover. There was nothing for the students to look up on the internet. If they wanted answers: there was a textbook, readings, and the professor to ask. Facebook could not possibly be a priority over learning. I figured they were paying enough to get an education, they better actually pay attention to their class. I was being paid enough I should have the liberty to decide if I wanted technological devices allowed in my classroom. It took me long enough to allow laptops and that was killing me. I didn't know if they were taking notes, streaming the internet, or if they were instant messaging. But I was told by the chair of the department to allow laptops, that much wasn't a choice.

Denny was here, but there was no light on his face like there usually was. He just stared ahead, exhausted, blank. I was concerned. He didn't put his phone in the basket, although I knew that he had it on him somewhere. He didn't say anything during class and usually he was very involved in discussion. I dismissed class and students streamed out like their pants were on fire. Denny moved slowly, shoving his notebooks forcefully into his knapsack. "How'd Saturday go?" I asked quietly, almost scared to ask considering the look on his face.

"I had to cancel on the recruiter." he breathed, looking down to his brown leather shoes. His face twisted nervously as he avoided eye contact.

"Could they reschedule?" I asked.

"I don't know, I don't know. I hope so." He slung his bag on his back. He was absolutely deflated.

"Would you like to get coffee later? It might lift your spirits." And defrost mine for God's sake.

"I'm not doing anything now." he replied looking up briefly. His words were slow and deliberate. Together we left the classroom and took the elevator to get downstairs. I was doing much better getting up the stairs than down, surprisingly. I didn't want to risk stairs right now though. All I wanted was to be able to keep up with this young man. I could tell he was slowing drastically so we could walk together. As soon as we reached the sidewalk outside I reminded myself: pick up one foot and set it down. Don't slide it across the concrete, you'll wear the soles of your shoes out too fast if you do that. Stand up straight, you look like you're ninety years old and homeless. Then I said out loud, "Look forward, not down. You'll never keep the respect you've earned if you don't look at the people coming towards you."

Denny suddenly looked up. The wind was picking up and he held onto the loose hat on his head. "Sorry."

"No, no, just some advice. What's got you so down?" I asked.

"It's just my sister."

"Bridget, right?" I held tightly onto my bag as if I was worried it would fly away. Denny was worried about his hat too; he held it down with his pale, skinny hand. The wind picked up quickly and shook every little twig surrounding us.

He nodded, and turned away as we walked up to the

coffee shop, also, annoyingly named after a tree: Mahogany Lawn. I was never sure what that meant or what the point of that was. It was here before I showed up. Denny held the door for me. We ordered and received our cups before sitting down. I had mine in a to-go cup for convenience. The people who worked at Mahogany Lawn knew that by now, though. I didn't have to order. All I had to do was swipe my card, smile, and sit down. We sat down at a table away from the window and near the heating vent. "Yeah, Bridget, she went to hospital Saturday morning."

"If I may ask, why?"

He shook his head and said, "She's had cervical cancer for over a year now. It's just not getting any better. They took her in because she reacted badly to one of her medicines. She's still in there now. They're doing tests to see if it's spread, the… the cancer I mean." He took in a deep breath and looked at his cup of coffee. It wasn't black, it was a creamy beige.

I honestly didn't know what to say that would help. "I'm sorry to hear that."

"You don't need to be sorry, you didn't do anything." He was avoiding eye contact. "You know, I don't even know why people say that." His voice was harsher than I was used to hearing from a student, but I couldn't expect anything differently. "My friend Mindy was in your class last year… well, um… and she heard the other history professors talking about your wife's death. What'd she die of?" More of that confusing, burning heat flooded my body. More hallucinations.

"Pancreatic cancer." I replied. "I guess I don't really have

have any comforting words for you. I apologize."

"How'd you cope?" he asked.

I shrugged and said, "I listen to the radio so there's always noise, or listen to my records, and I've done my work and my research. It's the best I can do." I didn't really cope. I hadn't gotten over her death. I still hadn't moved past my son's death either.

"I just wish I could fix it…" he muttered. "I wish that there'd be some kind of miracle."

"You can't fix it." I said and looked him briefly in the eye. "And don't put the burden on your shoulders to fix it. It's a biological thing, you can't wish it away."

"That doesn't mean I can't try." He laughed sadly, scratching the back of his head.

"And that doesn't mean it's harmless to think you can change it." I said sternly. "You have a responsibility to take care of yourself. I know what its like to dote and expend all your energy on something that isn't going to change because of your efforts. You fretting and stewing over this isn't going to help your sister, especially if she knows about it, because then she knows that you're hurting because of her."

"What do I do then?"

"Be supportive, but not overbearing." I replied. "That's all I can tell you."

He took a sip of his coffee and said, "I live with my sister. It's my job to fret, plus I can't bear to see her struggle like this. She's up so many nights because of the pain. She cries so much. I feel like it's my job to make it better."

I smiled and said, "You're a good brother, Denny. You can help, to an extent, like I mentioned, but don't neglect yourself in the time being. Bridget knows about your school, and the scholarship opportunity. See if you can get that rescheduled. I'm sure she wants to see you earn it."

He laughed again and said, "She was mad when I stayed with her at the hospital on Saturday, said I should leave so I could make rehearsal." He looked down at his cup and his eye brows lifted up quickly and then back down, his entire face changing in the process before settling down to a resting position.

"Next time, listen to her." We paused and drank our coffee. I was finally defrosting. "So you went to boarding school?" I asked, hoping to lighten the mood.

"Ah, yeah, I was a boarding school brat." He smiled, lightening up a bit. "And one hell of one at that."

"What does that mean?"

"Bridget said I was over involved, at least in the theater. I'm not much of a fan of being around lots of people unless I'm pretending to be someone else."

I cocked my head to one side. "That sounds like a problem."

He shrugged and took another sip of coffee. "I've been told I'm not much of a personality. So I guess it's nice that I can just step inside the shoes of someone who is already fully realized, and even extremely different from who I am, it's fun. It makes it easier to talk to people even if it's scripted. Like with Hamlet, I wouldn't normally go so crazy and kill people." I was glad to see him smile. He was lightening up just a bit. He rubbed his chin for a moment before putting his hands back on his cup for warmth.

I nodded slowly, laughing. "Good to know…still sounds

like something to be concerned about."

"Eh, I had a teacher tell me that meant I was in the right field of work." He laughed too and looked down at the cup. "I heard it's like the same with writers. A lot of writers say they write because they can't help it. They have to do it, or they'll go crazy. Other people say that what they write down is really like the voices in their head. I'm assuming that means they're in the right field of work too. That teacher I mentioned suggested I should start working musicals and stuff because I get really into musicals. I like to sing."

"Are you a show tunes freak too?" He nodded. "Wow…"

"Uh huh. Yeah… one day I want to move to Los Angeles, I think it would be easier to find work there, at least for the screen." He shrugged and leaned back in his chair comfortably.

"Oh God, don't move there."

"Really?"

"Yes, I'm not kidding." I said. "It's not worth it. The people there are…uh, freaks, or at least there are a lot of freaks there. You don't want to waste your breath, or your time and energy. There's plenty of work over on this side of the continent, I assure you. Or if you go back home you can get work there."

"And be stuck in Shakespeare for the rest of my life?" he asked. "They hear this accent and that's what I'm stuck doing."

"I doubt the only work for you is Shakespeare."

"That's not what I was thinking." he replied indignantly. "And Shakespeare is so depressing, even the comedies are depressing."

"Isn't that the essence of life?" I asked, breaking a smile once again.

He smirked a bit and said, "People go to a show to get lost in it, as an escape. I think I should be in it for the same reason, even if it does drive me into exhaustion and kill me slowly in the process."

"That's what I don't understand about theatre people. You always complain about how much work it is, but you keep going back." There was a light that came into his eyes and he looked behind him briefly as he had been doing every once in a while since we came in this building. He always acted as if there'd be someone behind him.

"I've been told it's kind of like childbirth. When it's happening you are thinking why the hell did I get myself into this? I'm never doing this again. This is going to kill me. What am I doing to my body? Why am I screaming so much? Then you look at the person nearest to you and scream, you did this to me!" He laughed. "Next thing you know it's all over and you are really happy, forget the pain, and then you miss it and it happens again."

"You miss the pain?" I asked, laughing. He was opening up so much, the smile on his face was genuine. I was glad I could lighten his mood up at least a little bit.

"It sounds rather masochistic, which is probably why all theater people are so odd… but no, it's probably something else we miss. Since we all go through hell and back together, it's unique." He shook his head and said,

"There are just things that can only happen during a play. And it's like what happens there stays there and never leaves because it's sacred or something. There are so many stories of people running up and down the halls without clothes on, or about how many children were conceived in the catwalk, or how many balloons were made out of condoms that were supposed to be used for microphone receivers and people sitting in corners eating animal crackers and fast food until they pass out. It's just how it works."

I was laughing so much at this point it hurt just about everything. "Young people."

"Don't say you didn't do wild stuff when you were younger."

"Not like that. I wasn't a theatre person."

"Ah, the losses." he replied. "Oh, and another fun thing is, at least with this production, I get to go on a lot of screaming rampages, it's rather soothing."

"You're insane." I replied.

"Yes, probably." He looked at his mostly empty cup. "And what makes the whole level of geekiness worse is I'm also into music."

"That wouldn't help." I said. "Not that it's a bad thing. What were you in?"

"Band and choir. I'm no good at playing instruments, like in orchestra or something. I've managed to pick up some things on the guitar and piano, just because they are so alike. I tried playing the bass for orchestra, but I don't know, it didn't work out. I stuck with it until uni though. I think I actually mentioned this to you at some point, but I was thinking about being a music major when I came to HBC.

Music performance or something like that, but I realized that I probably wasn't going to make any money doing that and gave up the boy band dream, or at least that's what my sister called it."

I laughed and shook my head. "You, in a boy band?" That was the last thing I could imagine him doing. There wasn't enough charisma in him to keep it going, he was too quiet, and he sure as hell couldn't pretend to be something else in that profession, if it could possibly be called that. His smile was contagious, though. I was smiling too. That was a rare sight. My face felt contorted in ways it really wasn't used to.

"Sort of." He shrugged. "It seemed like a real possibility at the time, which is stupid to think about. I also contemplated being in a professional symphony, which sounds much better. My parents didn't like either idea, and I liked acting more so I went with that. Although choir is just as interesting of an experience as being around theater people. There's that same feeling of comradery."

"Apparently."

"And about that project I'm supposed to be working on... that's just..."

"Understandable." I interjected. "Although I better the hell see a final project come the end of the semester or you aren't graduating. You've come in enough to speak about it, I'm sure you're doing alright."

"I know, I know." he said, shaking his head. "I'm working on it the best I can. Once hell month for the play, is over, it'll be on the top of the to-do list."

"Has hell month just started?"

"There's three weeks left. We open next week." His eyes lit up. "You should come and see the play. Students and faculty get in free. You can see me go absolutely barmy."

"I don't know what you just said."

"Crazy. Insane. You know, nuts." he replied, his smile growing just a bit brighter. "My sister uses that word a lot."

Chapter Five

Misery in the sound of the wind
In the sound of a few leaves
Which is the sound of the land
Full of the same wind
That is blowing in the same bare lace
For the listener, who listens in the snow
And nothing, himself, beholds,
Nothing that is not there,
And nothing that is.
(Wallace Stevens)

I looked out my office window. This winter was oddly snowy. The snow was white and fluffy, landed on the ground evenly until the wind picked up the flakes in swirling clouds which appeared like twisters. When the wind died, the snow would settle again and the air would become clear. The early evening light clung to the white snow and made it glow.

I had coffee in front of me as always and listened to Katja Kellogg outside the office speaking with Dr. Rogers. Both stayed late today, working on their respective projects. Katja was an interesting young woman, with an equally interesting voice to match. It had a comfortable pace which swayed as she spoke. The young woman was hired just three years ago, fresh out of grad school as a professor in Eastern European History. She was a nice girl; her parents were immigrants from Ukraine who came here during the Cold War. She brought me lunch a few times since Tess died. I couldn't hardly look at her anymore, though. There was a well of pity in her eyes, just screaming to remind me I was sick. She'd leave a little 'get well' notes on my desk, covered in bright, colorful stickers... as if I could get well.

I looked back outside. The lights of the chapel were on, reaching into the ever-darkening sky. I only walked in that place once a year, for Christmas Vespers. Tess dragged me there since the first year we lived here. She loved Christmas, thought it was the best time of year. She loved every aspect of it, the snow, the presents, the cookies, the craziness, the family, and the churchiness too. I would give in once a year to join her at church and that was Vespers.

The snow outside didn't look horrible. I really didn't hate snow all that much, only what it stood for. Winter. I didn't like winter. Never had. This, though, looked like Christmas snow, the good kind. It wasn't the wet heavy snow that could be made into anything, but it was the unnaturally light snow that made funny noises when walked on. It snowed like this the last Vespers Tess and I went to. It was also the last real outing Tess ever took. She was so excited to go. She was in a wheelchair at that time, extremely weak, emaciated really. But she wore her favorite sweater that looked massive on her, her shoes wouldn't fit on her tiny little feet, and her favorite necklace over shadowed her.

She wore too much perfume that day too. I honestly think she was trying to cover up the smell of death that just hung over her. She wore those horrible tinted old people glasses too, but she was trying to cover up the jaundice in her eyes. Her eyes became a yellowish mess that wouldn't let me see the right color of blue in her anymore. She was fully aware, though, of how she looked, but this was her favorite thing in the world.

She and I rolled into the chapel, very early so we could make sure she got one of the handicapped spots. We were going to the Sunday night show, which was usually filled with old people, and thus, there was the risk of not getting the seats we needed. Just as always there were ushers that showed us to our seats, all wearing their Sunday best. It was a miracle that Tess convinced me to even wear a tie. At that point I was just so tired that I wasn't taking very good care of myself, and she made it clear that I had to be in tip-top shape to be out in public. I could have made any number of comments in return, but kept my mouth shut.

There were always students of mine that performed. I remembered that Denny was one of them. I think for every year he'd been at this school he sung "O Holy Night." Tess cried when she heard it, always did. She said it was the most beautiful thing in the world. It was her favorite Christmas song since she was a child. I was dry eyed and trying to distract myself by analyzing the clothing of the kids in front of me. I looked at the dresses on these girls, wishing that they just had a sense of decency and respect. Loose and heavy cleavage pouring out of low hanging dresses… it wasn't ok. Other girls were dressed like they thought they were nuns. At least those prudent girls weren't burning my eyes with things that I shouldn't be seeing. Some boys went up there looking like they had just woken up and dragged their asses there without even consulting hygiene.

After the next year though, Tess wasn't there to tell me to go to Vespers. I went anyways knowing what she would've wanted. I didn't go for the church aspect. I always felt like a hypocrite listening to the preaching with my mind closing against it, building a wall. My heart pounded with anxiety hearing the words. I just wanted to pretend like something was normal. In December, when I went alone, I arrived early, and sat right behind the handicapped section. I brought one of Tess's scarves in my pocket and I put it on the chair next to me. I watched as the stage was set up by the students.

I came alone with the intention of staying alone, but soon my students started to sit around me. It felt like it was out of pity, but I was happy to have the company and conversation. I even bowed my head when the prayers came like Tess always made me do. I never understood why people did that. Even when I did believe in God, I knew he wasn't down at my hands, he was somewhere else, like in the air, up in the sky, something... but I did it anyways. I tried to listen to the chaplain speak. He, though, had an oddly Southern Baptist flare in the inflections of his voice, and the loud bellowing and intensity of his words I simply couldn't swallow. My ears were closing. Yet other students were reading too, many of them, their voices were quiet, scared, meek.

I tried to swallow the whole virgin birth idea, the whole

first section of John about how the Word was with God and the Word was God, but I couldn't wrap my mind around it, never could. I wondered what Tess thought about it. She was always quiet in her faith around me. We were both conflict avoiders and didn't bring it up, just like politics. We each just stayed in our separate corners of the topics. Yet I knew she never wore a cross on her neck, she wore a dove. The dove had three sections to it, like the Trinity, and it was pointing downwards. She grew up in a Lutheran environment although the Trinity did seem to have a Calvinist flare to it. She just said she didn't like wearing a cross; it was a symbol of human stupidity, and it was an instrument of Roman death and torture… she didn't like wearing it around her neck. She knew fully well what it symbolized, but a dove was a symbol of peace.

There were no crosses in this building, nor stained glass. The only symbol that showed that it was a church was the giant Dutch organ in front of me. It hung above the stage, illuminated by the ceiling lights. It was intimidating in a way. It's sound shook me to the core, but at the same time the sound of the organ was oddly comforting. It was Tess's favorite instrument. She always thought "Toccata and Fugue in D Minor" was the most gorgeous piece ever written, past her obsession for "O Holy Night".

The first music I heard was from this massive instrument. Its sound came rushing at me with surprising force, and I was caught off guard. I could just barely see the player of this instrument. He was a student who would graduate that May. He sat up straight, and the only hint I could tell who it was, and that it was Dr. Roger's son was because of the back of his head. He had his father's perfect, almost naturally grey blonde hair which he kept at an acceptable length, unlike his father's ratty ponytail.

The choir began to sing after the organ quieted; and they sang from behind in the balcony, singing church Latin, until they switched into what I believed to be Swahili. The voices just broke this most unholy silence in me and I almost cried. It was gorgeous. It was real and it was human. It wasn't an instrument just blowing air through it, these were breathing and living human beings. I felt almost embarrassed by the emotions I felt but I knew that Tess would have loved it.

As the night went on, it wasn't getting any better, my emotions at least. I was overwhelmed. I knew that "O Holy Night" was coming up and I wasn't sure if I was going to get through it without breaking. Up stepped the full choir and Denny with a girl beside him. I'd never seen her before, but they were wearing matching attire, both with navy blue and black, her a dress with black tights, and him with a blue shirt, wrinkled of course, and a crooked tie. They began quietly, calmly, but I thought I was going to fall down on the line "Fall on your knees", but as they quieted again, the organ came on, and so did the full choir. I was choking. I held onto the arms of the chair. Tess would be crying right now, out of happiness. I hadn't cried since she died. I wasn't going to cry because of a stupid song… but it was gorgeous, every note, every line was seeping into me just like that imaginary burning that plagued me so terribly.

The organ ceased to play and it was just the voices, beautiful, harmonic, perfect voices singing… I supposed I could have been dead at that moment and not known it. While she was living, Tess spoke about the choirs of angels in Heaven, maybe they really were singing, and if they sounded as good as this, maybe sitting in clouds for eternity wouldn't be that boring. I supposed she was greatly enjoying hearing divine music if that was what was going on, if that was where she was.

After Vespers, going into the house, I was painfully aware of the sudden, deafening silence. Titan was fast asleep, snoring even, on his big pillow like bed near the fireplace that never seemed to have fire in it anymore. I hung up my coat, but didn't say "I'm home." There was no point. I stepped into the kitchen and poured myself a big glass of wine and sat down in my armchair and just breathed. Tess was on my mind. She was always on my mind this time of evening. Right now, she'd be telling me to take my shoes off, they aren't allowed to be on the carpet. She'd tell me that it's not proper to have the bottle of wine next to me. She'd say that this wine was for guests only, not my own personal drinking habits. She'd be standing right in front of me telling me not to be sad. She had said it to me over and over again while she was sick. She kept saying she loved me but she knew how I was going to react to her being gone and she didn't want me to be sad. She told me I needed to pull myself up from my bootstraps and keep on trudging on through this jungle. She told me to be the Marine I used to be. She told me to be the man she married. Of course, I didn't listen to any of that. It wasn't like her saying it made it miraculously possible. She believed in miracles, but a miracle didn't save her from that disease and a miracle sure as hell wasn't going to save me from Parkinson's. Miracles weren't real. Tess told me she was happy that she got to see Benjamin soon, our son. That was her miracle.

It was then I remembered the day we heard Ben died. We drove to the funeral home and the place that makes gravestones. I was quiet the entire time; my jaw was locked tight with anger, and it flew through me like it was blood and like it was natural. But it was corrosive, and I could feel it eating away at my stomach, my heart, my throat, and my brain. It was difficult to breathe. It was the same feeling I had when I heard Denny singing last Vespers.

Tess wore her floral skirt that was all pastel colors, but had faded so badly that flowers couldn't even be picked out on it. She looked older than she should have with the worry wrinkles on her face, but she stood tall like she owned the world even if she disagreed with it for a little while. I opened the door and she walked in. There was a receptionist at a desk who was very young, not in much danger of dying if she wasn't in a war zone. Her hair was in that odd nineties style where it wasn't as big as the 80's but still too big for it to look nice. The dollar store gel clinging to it was disgusting and a distraction, and so was the purple lipstick that clung to her teeth. She smiled at us and said, "How may I help you?"

If I was going to speak I'd say, "We need your help burying our son. He got blown to bits over in the Gulf."

But instead Tess was smart enough to talk first. Her voice was only slightly shaky. "We need to buy a headstone and… and an urn for our son. Do you have anyone available to help us?"

"Yes ma'am, if you could fill out this form right here." The young woman had an annoying southern accent that sounded fake. Tess took the clipboard with the black pen that was attached by a chain. Who the hell was going to steal a pen from a funeral home? We sat down in the awkward waiting area that was completely silent.

Tess filled it out, also in silence. That was probably for the best. I was still too angry to really function. I just held my hands on my knees and tried to calm myself via breathing techniques Tess taught me, but they really weren't helping all that much. We returned the form to the young woman and were led past a door to a man who looked like he belonged in this profession although I wasn't sure why. He wore an oddly light-colored grey suit that looked like the skin of a dead man, but a yellow shirt underneath of it that was the pastel yellow of my wife's skirt. His tie was white though. It didn't make sense and it looked a few sizes too big for him. I couldn't detect an age on him. "Hello, how may I help you?" Same damn words that young lady gave. Shivers went through me at his smooth tone. "I'm Thomas."

"Hello, Thomas, can we look... can we look at your gravestones?"

"Of course, of course, let me take you to our display room." It made me so angry that these people were making money off death. I always thought it would be better if we could just be put in the ground as is and let nature do as it wished. At least Ben wasn't embalmed like some mummy and stuck in a coffin like he was alive and left to stay like that for a while and then rot, inside some silk lined hunk of metal. But right now, he was in a wooden box right next to a triangle shaped flag, also in a wooden box, but a better wooden box. There was more respect for that damned flag than my own son's life. We needed something better for his remains to be in and under. We sat down at a table with wooden chairs, probably pine… and he gave us a catalog and sat in front of us. "What were you two thinking? Something joint or…"

"No, no, this isn't for us." I stated. I could feel Tess tense up just at my speaking. "This is for our son."

He nodded, and said, "What type of stone would you like?" He proceeded to list off names.

Tess looked at me and said, "Benjamin, he told me he didn't want anything fancy in case something happened. He just wanted his name, the dates, and then that he was in the Army and… he had a quote that he liked… it's by Mae West, I… I remember it, it's 'You only live once, but if you do it right, once is enough.'" She smiled and wrote it down on a piece of paper. "Can that be put on the stone?"

"Of course it can ma'am, but what style of stone are you thinking?" She pointed at a color, probably the simplest one there was and then she wanted his full name to be on there: Benjamin Henry Basilla, then the dates, his rank, awards… and then that damned quote they both thought was a good idea. We picked up just a straightforward rectangular stone that stuck upwards. She looked at me and said, "We could pick one out now for us?"

"Tess…" I mumbled.

"Neal, we have the money and it is easier just to get it done now."

"Where are we supposed to put the damn thing?" I asked.

"When we buy Ben's plot, we can just get the one next to it for us and put the stone there too, after his service and all."

"Don't you think that's a bit weird, having our names in a cemetery when neither of us are dead yet?"

The man across the table said, "We can hold it for you, if you like. No extra charge."

"See, Neal." She made eye contact. "Come on, let's pick one out." I didn't say much, just nodded and brought out the checkbook when the time came. She wanted a double one, our names on the same stone. She picked out everything. She was more enthusiastic than I and I really didn't want to see my name on a stone until the necessary time came, or never.

But it was a good idea because when Tess got sick I didn't have time to do any of that. I was driven literally bonkers, or as Denny said: barmy. After Tess died, it was the oddest feeling I ever experienced. It wasn't just because she wasn't there anymore, but I wasn't feeding her, cleaning her, giving her medicine, going to doctors, to meetings. She died that summer, so I had some time before going back to school and it was the worst emptiness I experienced in my life. It was because of that stress that the worst symptoms of my own disease caught up to me. I went to the doctors immediately; I'd been on the medicine for a while, but I wasn't able to think straight, and felt awful. There were times when I would just completely freeze up. They said that the levodopa was giving me some kind of brain toxicity and they would just put me on anti-depressants. They told me not to drink while I was on them.

But here I was in my chair, drinking. I didn't really care about what the doctor said anymore. They were just pumping me full of chemicals anyways. Nothing was helping. Every damn medication they tried failed, or caused worse damage than the disease by itself. I didn't trust the doctors much anymore, which was odd because Benjamin wanted to be a doctor. He thought it would be amazing if he could help people. He thought he could change the world that way. He was always into learning and living things. He always asked me why I liked dead things. I never really thought about it before, but he wished to focus his energy on the life that was already there, what was in front of him, living, breathing, what could be helped and saved while I was focusing on what already happened, what was done and over, and people who were no longer alive. I thought it was important, just as much as he thought the work he would do was important.

Chapter Six

I couldn't pass up an opportunity to see Denny go absolutely bonkers. I needed something to distract me. The last performance of Hamlet was going to be Sunday afternoon, after an entire week of nightly performances. I could only imagine how exhausted the cast and crew were from the past few months of work. Yet I supposed the Sunday afternoon showing was so old people could come. At least that was the stigma attached to it. So I, as an old person, decided to attend this performance. The auditorium was pretty packed as soon as I arrived, and so I sat near the aisle in the center. I didn't want to be too far back I couldn't see, but if I was in the front, and around a lot of people, I could be a distraction because of my hands and legs. After choosing my seat carefully, I sat down while the lights were still up. I was surprised by the number of students in attendance. More than half of the auditorium seats were filled.

The show started on time and immediately I was impressed by the scenery presented to me. There was a staircase built in the center, and windows flanking it on either side. Both expressed extreme detail. It was all hand painted. I could only imagine the work, and fun that was poured into the making of what I saw. Someone cared about what was put on stage. Soon, though, I realized that I wasn't horribly interested in the plot in comparison to the set and costume designs until Denny come out on stage. I wanted to laugh, in a good way. He just looked like he belonged there too well and yet for some reason it was odd to see him in the situation he was in. I saw the reason he grew his hair out. It was in a ponytail, only to be let loose later when he'd go mad. He wore very simple, black, sophisticated clothing and stood, walked, and spoke with great confidence. I'd never seen him so sure of himself before. Although, truly, I was very thankful that there wasn't a strict guideline of Elizabethan dress going on, I wouldn't have been able to take anything seriously. The Shakespearian language was already rather over the top for me, but I could follow it well enough, but Denny was the only one that didn't have to fake a terrible accent. Everyone else sounded awful.

All I could expect from this point onwards was the cliché 'to be or not to be speech' followed by dying, lots, and lots of dying. A great deal of the acting was very stiff, almost annoying. This school, of course, was not known for its theatre department. It was a reasonably good program but not great, had a good building, and good equipment and good faculty, it just didn't have many good actors. I was beginning to wonder why the hell Denny even decided to come to this school if he wanted to be a theatre major. But being as he intended on being a music major coming in, I understood. HBC had one of the best music programs around, and was one of the strongest, most well-respected school. Denny made a good decision, though, it was better to be one major or the other rather than both if he wanted life and sanity. Maybe he felt that path was inadequate and decided to follow his affinity for history and take it up as a minor. It was a smart move, the history part at least.

When Polonius spoke, I laughed my ass off. That man was an actor, he was convincing me that he was a weird, probably drunk, creepy old man who disturbingly reminded me of myself. I wasn't that funny, but he walked with such a lurch and oddly robotic motions and I was sure that to some people I probably looked like that. My speech slurred sometimes, so I probably sounded drunk. The beard he had was reminiscent of the one I had three years ago before stress started eating away at my hair, both on top of my head and on my chin. Denny's acting wasn't at all robotic or unbelievable either. So much so that I kind of was concerned about him when he started going mad. It didn't seem much like acting anymore. He screamed about how horrible of a human being he was saying, "What an ass am I?" That was going to stick in my head forever.

A strong, smirk smeared his face. His hair was now loose from the perfect ponytail that was behind his head originally and was now disheveled and his eyes were bulging out enough that I could see that there really was eyeliner on them. The look he held was intense, burning, unnatural for Denny. That to be or not to be speech was coming up and I was really interested in seeing it. But after all that screaming, how could he possibly do that? I'd be exhausted enough to need a three-hour nap.

It did come, and he was sitting on a platform, his feet

not hitting the floor and they were swinging back and forth, childishly. His voice was very calm, quiet, and melancholy to begin with. He held a cloth doll in his hand. The further into the speech he got, he dug his fingers into the doll, pulling it apart. His hands were trembling in anger. I only wished mine would stop. I was amazed by the smoothness of his voice. It seemed so real that I just wanted to run up there and tell him that it would be ok.

After the third act there was a sizeable intermission. The curtain came down and the lights went up. People stood up from their seats and filed into the lobby to get refreshments. I didn't want to risk trying to get up and back in time. My brain was already turning to mush from too much thinking. It was true that a person was a garden, and after a certain amount of neglect it would thorn over and die. I felt those thorns all over myself, but they weren't going to go away with a set of scissors. They were going to choke me, that I was well aware of. I couldn't make sense of hardly anything.

The auditorium was almost empty, although there were some students congesting the walkway in clumps like cholesterol. There was a girl who came out from behind the curtain. She was wearing all black and I assumed she was part of the crew. She had her hair in a neat bun, and there was a warm smile on her face, although she did look as tired as anyone would be if they had been subjected to the same hell as what this production was described as. "Hi, I'm Mindy, I was in one of your classes about two years ago. Denny asked me to give these to you." she said, handing me a bottle of water and a brownie. I was sure I had her in class before, she looked terribly familiar.

I smiled and said, "Tell him thank you for me. I brought him some snacks."

"He really isn't allowed to eat in costume." she replied.

"Then put a bib over him or something. That man has been screaming for like two hours, he must be hungry." I laughed and handed her one of the paper bags that I brought.

"Will do. Enjoy the rest of the show, sir." The very image of Denny, wearing that prince's costume, however disheveled he looked, with a bib on, would be hilarious. As people came back inside, the noise level rose and then fell as the lights did the same.

The next two acts were probably my favorite. Hamlet was firmly established as wacky, Ophelia went nuts too, and then I was oddly relieved when Polonius was killed by Hamlet. Although seeing Denny with a sharp dagger was rather odd, especially when he planned on killing his praying step-father just before that, and I thought he was going to do it.

Yet by far I loved the gravediggers most; the ones who were making Ophelia's grave. They looked and sounded like they were going to be stupid, but they said the most wonderful things in the entire play. I was just sad they didn't last longer. Then when Laertes and Hamlet were sword fighting, although it was more like fencing, they both apparently managed to get wounded enough to die; I was impressed that either of them could fence. Or even handle a sword and not look hilariously awkward. Denny always seemed like he was rather clumsy to me and here he was, light on his feet, stabbing people.

It seemed like too easy of an end for a play, but it was Shakespeare and it was a tragedy. It had been almost twenty years since reading Hamlet, and I supposed that nothing remained in my memory to use as a reference except an image of the cover of the book I read- a gaunt, skeletonized young man with thinning hair looking down to a skull while wearing a green turtleneck.

After the lights went up again I waited for people to leave before I got up. I used a cane I dug out of my closet for some extra support. I had to keep it firmly on the ground as much as possible or it would start waving madly in the air. If Tess knew I'd need to use a cane, she would have bedazzled it herself. However, the lurch was worse today than usual. I was beginning to be shaped like a younger Stephen Hawking.

I wanted to congratulate Denny on such a perfor-mance. He deserved it. So I shuffled out, some of the other actors were already out in the lobby, and there were crew members taking microphone packs from their pants or dresses, which was rather odd, but no one hardly seemed to notice. I congratulated some of them, and I was looking for Polonius as well.

I found a bench and sat down, looking at the crowd. I was disappointed with how exhausted I was and it was only six in the evening. I took a drink from the water bottle I'd been given and tried to sit still. Denny did come out of the back room and waved at me, made some rounds and came back. He wasn't in costume, mostly. He washed his face off, put glasses on, and was wearing sneakers despite the breeches or something resembling breeches he was wearing as pants.

"Did you get the cookies I sent with Mindy?" I asked.

"Yes, and I ate them." He nodded, laughing. "Thank you, I didn't know you could bake."

"Well, I can't. I bought them at the grocery store. I hope they're ok." I said. "You did a very, very good job up there."

"Guess who came tonight." He seemed really happy. "The scout from the university. I wasn't able to find him afterwards, but I'm sure I will hear from him soon."

"I'm glad he came tonight; you went absolutely mad up there." I laughed again.

"Yes, and every night I seem to give myself a headache from that." He rubbed his forehead and sat down next to me. "And exhaust myself. I suppose it takes a lot of energy to be crazy."

"Of course." I took in a deep breath.

Polonius came and sat down next to Denny. "Congratulations on your performance." I said and shook his hand.

"Why thank you."

"You acted like a drunk." Denny said, his eye brows raising.

"That's because I am." He laughed. "I don't do this show without something in me." He patted his stomach. "It's not genuine otherwise."

"That would explain the smell." Denny touched his shoulder. "It was a pleasure killing you every night for however long it has been."

"And it has been a pleasure making sure my daughter doesn't get any pleasure from you..." He yawned and stretched. "I will see you tomorrow for strike."

He stood up and walked crookedly towards the exit. "Drunk? Really?" I asked.

"He learned his lines drunk, can't seem to recite them sober." Denny said. "I do need something to drink though."

I pulled out a bottle of wine I brought with me as a gift. His eyes opened widely. "How does this look?" I asked.

"Damn." he replied. "I really need that right now."

"Well I'm going home for dinner if you would like to join me. It's quiet. I'm planning to make spaghetti for dinner."

"Sounds wonderful." he replied. "I need food. Give me a second, I need to get my bag. Would you mind if Mindy joined us? I was going to drive her home."

"And you are thinking of drinking?" I asked.

"She can drive to her house and my apartment is a block away from hers so, I'll be alright." He promised and ran off.

Once we got to the house, I was just happy there were people actually there for a change. It seemed like a home for a little while. The dogs stood up and greeted the two with excitement, more than they'd shown in a long time. Titan seemed a bit slower than usual but he wasn't doing so well these days. Age caught up to him with a vengeance. His medicine was keeping him up and walking for the most part, but there was still a lot of pain in his eyes. I'd been filling up the bathtub with warm water most days and he could just lay in it and relax. It seemed to give him enough solace, that, and he would hog half the bed at night.

I brought over wine glasses. Mindy said she didn't drink but I had sparkling grape juice on hand which seemed festive enough. There was too much wine saved up in my cellar, and I didn't drink very much, so I didn't want it to go to waste. I wanted it to go to someone and enjoyed.

Denny sipped on it immediately, calming down like a baby with a bottle. We were talking about frivolous topics, the kids sharing more antics about what happened behind set. Mindy said she worked every single show in this college since she was a freshman. She had even volunteered here three years prior to that as well. She enjoyed the theater but never acted. "I hate acting. Too many people looking at me, I can't remember any of the lines. I can do improv though."

"You only play crazy people then." Denny sighed, his words were already beginning to slur. He rubbed the back of his neck almost incessantly like he really couldn't help it. If he wasn't doing that, his face twisted in odd contortions, or his jaw was going back and forth nervously. I didn't know why he acted so odd, whether it was the alcohol or the girl.

"Says you."

"Yes, says me." Denny said sternly. "I think I have a right to judge how mad a person is going."

"Yes, that is true." she replied and yawned.

"You cannot possibly be getting tired." he said, cocking his head to the side and then to the other, a few times over. He stared blankly at the wine glass and began twirling the dark red liquid around before taking another sip. I think he had at least half the bottle just to himself by the time he finished the spaghetti.

"I've been sleep deprived for two months. I'm tired."

"That's what caffeine is for!" Denny exclaimed.

"It makes me sleepier though!" she whined in response. "It doesn't work."

"Then you're just weird." he stated finally. I was laughing, trying to finish off my own spaghetti. He poured another glass. I knew I probably should cut him off, but I was entertained. We ate with odd conversation inbetween while we were all stuffing our faces full of spaghetti, acting oddly either because of wine or because of sleep deprivation. I told Denny he could take the rest of the wine home; he probably needed it. There was only a little at the bottom anyways.

"I need to keep this away from my sister when she gets home. Her and wine," He shook his head disapprovingly. "Not a good combination, she'll drink it right out of the bottle. Not much of a lady."

Mindy shook her head and said, "There's not going to be any left in the bottle by the time you get home mister. Come on."

He walked out, swaying back and forth, although he hadn't been walking in straight lines after his third glass of wine. Mindy held him by the shoulders, directing him to the car and onto the passenger seat. She waved at me and thanked me for a good dinner. Denny said something like a goodbye as well.

Chapter Seven

I sat in the cafeteria. It was Tuesday. I had some macaroni and cheese on my plate with some broccoli on the side. I stared it, wondering if my appetite would show up if I looked at good food long enough. If the cafeteria could make anything well, it was macaroni and cheese. The broccoli was properly steamed, not boiled, thankfully. I poked at it with my fork, and sighed. I sat next to the large window that encompassed two walls of the entire mess hall. The other two walls had food being served on them. I was in a booth that had red seats and new white tables that looked almost sterile although with all these university students around, I doubted it. I took in a deep breath and looked up. Denny was jumping up and down waving at me from behind the glass wall where the line of students waiting to get in formed. Confused, I waved back, wondering why he was so excited. "Hey Dr. Neal!" he yelled as he went through the entrance. No one seemed to notice his loud voice. I waved back, surprised by his exuberance.

As he filled up his cup with chocolate milk there were some boys from Red Oak dorm stacking their cups, one on top of the other until it was very, very tall. It was a joke to see who would end up with it and have to take it into the dish return conveyer belt. As long as Red Oak men were here, it could last all night. People knew well enough to sit with their hands on the rim of the cups if it was below a fourth full. My cup was full now, and so I didn't have to worry about that. I just had to worry about getting it to my mouth and swallowing.

Denny sat down across from me. He looked oddly happy. "Hi!" he jeered.

"What's got you so cheery?" I asked.

"Is it a bad thing?" he asked.

"Are you still drunk?"

"No, no, no, see that's why I don't drink that often, although I don't like beer and I can't afford the good wine and I only really like the good wine..." He was talking quickly and began eating his grilled cheese sandwich. "Are you not hungry?" he asked me, pointing at my food.

"Not really." I said.

"I'm really excited about tonight. My sister is making me some French onion soup." He smiled brightly and bit into his food. "My favorite soup."

"You and French things."

"It's soup, Dr. Neal. Just soup, although do you like anything at all about the French? Their art? Rococo art is pretty cool."

"You really are drunk." I said.

"No, no, no I'm not. I'd pass a sobriety test."

I raised my eyebrows. "Why don't I believe you?"

He laughed and said, "I guess I act drunk when I'm really happy."

I paused for a little while. "I still don't believe you."

His eyes went up and he jumped a bit as if something startled him. If he was drinking his milk, he would have choked. I wouldn't have been the only one choking. "Well… there was this girl."

"Oh, is that so?"

"Onto French art… Rococo, that's what I mentioned right?" he said, laughing.

"Tell more," I laughed.

His brow furrowed and a smirk formed on his face. "Someone's not sounding very proper."

"Someone got drunk at my house, and drank a bottle of sixty-dollar wine… the whole bottle." I began to eat my macaroni, trying to keep the fork from causing my food to fly all over the place. I went one damn noodle at a time.

"Fine…" he mumbled. "But no French art?"

"I hate impressionism. It's annoying and pointless." I said.

"I said rococo art. It's cool! It's exciting and passionate and colorful! The palace of Versailles is rococo architecture and that's breathtakingly beautiful! It's like the third reboot of classical art. I've seen it in person!"

"You need to slow down. I know what the hell rococo art is Denny." I said. "And it's over detailed, there is randomly naked people, non-biologically correct musculature. It's so damn glittery that it's painful to look at. It's the most French thing in existence, their way of thought and everything. Seriously, have you seen the portrait of Louis XIV?"

"Of course." He was still smirking. He was red like a Beef Master tomato.

"That man is wearing tights, high heels and a couple hundred dead mink. It's ridiculous."

"It's what they wore back then."

"It's what the damned French wore back then." I stated strongly. A noodle went flying off my fork and landed on the window and stuck there. I closed my eyes for a moment, wishing that didn't happen.

Denny laughed and shook his head, "Impressive, Dr. Neal. Impressive. Louis XIV was a cool guy."

"Really? That man was as queer as a three-dollar bill."

"I have never heard that expression in my entire life…" he said, still laughing.

"Well, in his case, it applies perfectly. That man had more voluminous hair than my wife did in the eighties, and that's saying something." I put my fork down, still slightly embarrassed by the flying noodle. I think I was too old to blush properly. Denny looked behind me and put his hand on his cup. Mine was still full.

"Those Red Oaks." he said. "They're annoying."

"Just like Louis XIV."

"Dr. Neal…" he mumbled. "You are the one here with issues. Do you like any other art? Caravaggio?"

I had to think for a moment. "He's not French, but first, why are you so interested in art?"

He shrugged and finished off the last of the chocolate milk and put the cup near the window so it was out of reach of any Red Oak. "I took some classes on art history, it was much more interesting than taking American history."

"Ain't that the truth… it's so boring!" I exclaimed.

"You like lived through half of it though."

"I'm not that old." I said heatedly. "I may be as old as dirt, but I didn't know George Washington, or even Woodrow Wilson. I'm sorry to disappoint." I laughed.

"But it's fun to look at art, there's a lot of detail and genius put into it. I like Caravaggio it's gorgeous in the way he used light. It is rather experimental."

"You should be speaking in the past tense. The man's dead."

"It was, there. Past tense."

"If I remember right he liked beheading people and painting pictures of half-dressed prepubescent boys holding fruit. Does that not sound concerning to you?" I asked, carefully stabbing another noodle with my fork.

"Well he was kind of a sensualist, so it makes sense." Denny shrugged and said, "I'm getting more milk." He ran over to the drink stand, skipping just slightly as he went. That young man was so odd… he sat down and took in a deep breath. "Just think about the time period though. It was at the end of the Golden Age of Spain and the early Renaissance."

I replied, "I supposed he wanted to kill Biblical figures in his work so much because of what just happened."

"What do you mean?"

"That period of history. Have you learned nothing at this school? Ahh… Phillip the Second I believe, don't hold it on me because I'm no modern historian, but they were going to go like destroy England because of Elizabeth I. She was a woman, technically an illegitimate heir because the Catholic Church didn't really annul Henry VIII's marriage to Catherine of Aragon...and so they were Anglican by then and Spain was powerful from not having gone through the Holy Wars like the rest of continental Europe for the past few hundred years... and they weren't going to let people be not Catholic and so were bent on destroying England. Unfortunately, most of the navy was destroyed in a freak storm that happened, nicknamed the Protestant Wind, because it only really hurt Spanish ships, not English ships, there went the Spanish navy and there went Spain's Golden Age."

His brow furrowed and he said, "You know too much."

"I suppose so, but the world was so odd then, so odd... he lived in the time of so much development, and interesting people like Bruno, Galileo, Bacon and Montaigne, God I hate Montaigne."

"Montaigne? Michel de Montaigne? You really do have issues with the French..." He shook his head. "This is serious. He's a pretty interesting read. We read him in a literature class."

"He's a big mouth and one of the only prisoners in the Bastille when it was stormed. It was stupid, they shouldn't have let him out. They should have left him there to suffer."

"Wow, you should see a doctor about this hate." Denny put his hands down on the table and made a very serious face for a moment.

"I don't like doctors and I don't like Montaigne." I said. His serious face broke.

His eyes lit up and he laughed. "Well I learned in that class that Montaigne's biggest fear seemed to have been to lose his ability to speak, and he died from like a tongue infection or something wrong with his tongue."

"That is wonderful. Perfect." I said.

"But, alright, Caravaggio, I really like him because he focuses on human subjects, he uses dark light, simple purposes and is able to make it look really realistic and beautiful."

"It's a lot of creepy looking boys with too much muscle for their age, open mouthed, deathly pale… I mean really, if you think I have problems, he must have even worse problems, and with all his biblical paintings… people in the Middle East aren't blonde… white, or red-headed and Mary is like fifteen and they make Joseph look like he's my age."

Denny laughed and said, "Well, you always stress in class to look at the context of the time period. They weren't that aware of what other people looked like and it would be odd for an artist to portray them as looking different than the way their patrons were expecting."

"The Spanish of all people should know something about diversity, they have been trying to destroy it for hundreds of years!" I laughed. "They tried that with the Muslims, now the Protestants, went to the Americas to wipe out the natives… yeah…" I shook my head and put my plate to the side.

"Dr. Neal you really need to eat more than that. There's some good cake over there if you want me to get you some." Why the hell was it his job to tell me when I needed to eat more? It wasn't like I could magically become hungry and magically be able to eat anyways.

"Sure." I sighed. I wasn't hungry. Cake would be interesting to eat. Sometimes it was still really cold here and would stay together better, but if it was very crumbly cake, it would get all over me and I didn't want to deal with that.

He brought over two pieces of cake and new forks regardless of the rant going on in my head. "Do you not want to use your other one?" I asked.

"It tastes like green beans." he simply replied. "One thing I do want to say about Caravaggio that I think you'd appreciate, is the Biblical figures he does portray are the ones like Thomas, Paul, and Peter and Mary Magdalen. They're the most interesting ones. Thomas is the doubter, the skeptic. Paul was a persecutor of Christians, he killed a lot of them until he became one. Peter was the one that kept denying Jesus and then running back to him over and over again, and they depict him being crucified upside down because he didn't think he deserved to die the way Jesus died. Mary Magdalen, some people thought she was a prostitute but most people just decided on the fact that she was a woman of 'ill repute'. I'm not sure what I think about that."

"I know who they are, I've taught an Early Christianity class for the past thirty-five years. But, I could just imagine how many disciples would have been lined up to be crucified just so they could die like Jesus…" I mumbled. "It must have been a common thing. Just a Roman form of execution that kind of… died out." I laughed at my own statement. Puns.

"Some people think the English did it at some point." Denny said, completely missing the funny thing I just said. Sigh. He stared at the cake on his fork, almost going cross-eyed.

"That's ridiculous they've been Christian since the 300's, on and off of course for a little while; the likelihood of them crucifying anyone is slim. Romans did that to Christians before they were Christian, but Christians wouldn't do that to Christians. That would be like an honor to them. Martyrdom was still a big deal to them at that point in time and for hundreds of years. It was the highest form of everything. If you died a martyr, you died a saint and you had this nice beautiful cult singing your name for all eternity. I'm sure that the Church did horrible punishments beyond that, but crucifixion… no, no, and no again. Plus there is no evidence to support it. None. Zip. Zero. *Nada*."

"You should eat that cake." Denny said. "It's really good."

"You haven't eaten yet either."

"That's because I'm waiting for you."

"Why?"

"I don't know." He ate the bit of cake that was on his fork and I did as well. It was getting caught in my throat a bit, it wasn't getting swallowed properly. I tried acting like nothing was going on. I tried to get a sip of my water, but my hand wouldn't hold the glass. "I think you need a straw; I'm going to go get one." And he did. Embarrassed, I drank out of the straw. "So I'm getting the drift that you don't really like the Spanish either?"

"Eh." I replied. "I don't really like a lot of people. They really drop out of history after the Spanish Golden Age after Phillip II, until the Spanish Civil War which didn't end that long ago, I was alive."

"It's such a rich culture, quite a nice place."

"Have you been there?" I asked.

"Yes, my parents took my Bridget and I to Barcelona." he said. "Wonderful culture, very different from English and American culture I think. At home, it seems like people are expected to be more restrained and careful in the way they present themselves. Over there flamboyance is the norm. People are hot blooded and loud. It's amusing."

"That might be why I don't like them." I said. "I don't handle people like that well. It was a trip getting used to my wife. She was so loud…" I mumbled and smiled. "She liked dancing and she was one of those… free spirits. She was English but came to study in America. Damn that woman went wacko once she got here. I'm sure you have heard about the movements going on in America at that time, especially in places like San Francisco."

"That's a Spanish word." he said. "But yes, when I had to take that American history course… I did learn about it. What was your wife's name?"

"Tess, Tess Lindel. She was from Bury St. Edmund's originally but said that the city was getting too commercial and so her family moved to Alnwick. When she was in Bury, not that Bury's all that big, she said she didn't like being around that many people. She was one of those people that likes to know everyone and everything about everyone."

"Was she a dancer?" he asked, sipping at the last of his second glass of milk.

"No, no, she was studying to be a nurse. She liked dancing, but she wasn't any good at it. I tried to teach her how to swing dance but that didn't go over too well. She wanted to lead, but didn't know how to, but the same went for me. I thought it would be romantic." I shrugged and sat on my hands briefly, wondering if that trick was ever going to work.

"My sister's a dancer." Denny said. "Well, she was. She can't dance right now. Went to school for it to. Together I think we destroyed our parents." He laughed. "They don't like artistic things. They expected her to be… I don't know a teacher or an engineer or a biologist. Almost anything but a dancer. She was really good at it though."

"So both of you like center stage? Sounds like a power struggle." I said.

"Nope, she's still much louder than I am. I'm only loud when I'm on the stage. She has a tendency to run the show, but I'm alright with that. I prefer when she runs the show actually, it's easier that way. Things have been changing in that dynamic since she's been sick though… she's not taking that very well."

"I've seen that myself as well, but she'll be alright with it. She needs to focus on getting better."

"She's well aware. It's just odd to see her like that, she's letting me make the decisions, and I have to take care of her. She fought so hard to do things herself at the beginning and the fact that she's just resigning to this is the most concerning part." He sat back in his chair and crossed his arms for a moment, nervously rubbing his arm.

"She's letting you help her. Allow that to happen, Denny. You can't fight it either." I said.

"I'm not, I'm not. I just… I just want her back to normal." he sighed and looked at the clock. "I have to go to my chemistry class." He looked at his phone. "And I have someone to call."

"Is that someone a girl?" I asked with raised eyebrows.

"Maybe."

"Is that girl the girl that you were skipping around about today?"

"How…? Ugh, yeah, maybe." He grinned widely, sheepishly too, and he was looking nervously around him.

"Ok, ok, have fun." I said and smiled. He grabbed my plates, cup and silverware and hopped off before I could say anything.

Chapter Eight

A very calm, rather good week went by. The weather was warming up and became acceptable as the month of March came. I appreciated the green coming up from the ground and was grateful for the sun. I never wanted to see winter again. I hated it so much. I even was doing well walking to school with Racer. He loved it. There was always so much to see and do. I relished the sunshine still, even if it didn't bring a perfect amount of heat.

I woke up in the morning to my alarm. I turned it off, fumbling to get the switch to go the right way. I patted Titan beside me. He'd been there all night, hadn't moved. As I touched him I was very concerned. I sat up and moved him, shook him. He still wasn't moving. "Titan?" I asked. No breath. No heart. Nothing. I didn't know what to do. I stared at him for a moment. He didn't look dead at all. He just looked like he was asleep, curled up like he always was to keep warm. His fur was still a little wet from when he lay in the bathtub last night. I shook him again, hoping that it was a trick, that he was smarter than me and wanted to scare me. Dogs don't do that. Dogs aren't that cruel. They are only cruel when they die.

Unable to think or process the information, I got out of bed and dressed, although my mind was frazzled and confused. I didn't know why I was reacting like this. I knew it was coming. He'd been ill for a while and it was for the best that he wasn't in pain anymore... but he had been around this house for so long, for nearly fifteen years. Racer was confused too when he tried to get Titan to come to breakfast with him. He didn't understand that the poor old dog wasn't going to be moving again. Racer's whimpering was terrible... awful... it made me feel ill.

I tried to continue my normal routine. I went off to the bathroom and filled my glass with water from the tap. I was nervous, normally my hands didn't shake for about half an hour after getting up, but they were beginning to. I took my medicine and tried to brush my teeth, but the tooth brush was flopping all over the place and I was getting the toothpaste all over my face... which meant that I had to clean it up, but I couldn't reach one of the smaller towels, so used a bath towel. That made me frustrated because I hated using messy bath towels. It was going to be impossible to wear a button up shirt today. I decided on a pullover sweater and some of those corduroy pants without any buttons. My shoes were a struggle to wear. On more than one occasion my doctor suggested I wear those crappy Velcro shoes that looked like they belonged on the homeless or people in nursing homes and I told her that while I still had a job I was going to look acceptably professional for it. That included not wearing crappy Velcro shoes.

I found the number for a pet cemetery that could pick him up and bury him for me. I was going to be at work, not here to see them carry him away. It probably wasn't acceptable to miss class because of a dog. But if I stayed, I'd cry. So I said goodbye to him before I took Racer out to go to school. There was no way I'd leave Racer alone with his dead brother. I couldn't seem to keep my mind straight. It was churning and running in circles. It was the oddest feeling of physical confusion. I could feel my mind not making the best of sense. I realized it probably wasn't the best idea to go out walking, but I needed it to help clear my mind. It wasn't only about Titan, though he triggered it. I was just too tired of all of this.

The sun was rather bright outside, although there were plenty of clouds crowding the sky. It was nice outside, I thought. That's good, that's good… now just act like the sun. Be all bright and cheery. Hell, when was I ever bright and cheery? I must be crazy to give myself that advice.

I held tight onto Racer's leash as we padded along the sidewalk. It was abnormally cold, but I didn't mind it. As long as there was sunlight. I walked along my usual path. I'd been walking the same path since I arrived over forty years ago. Many things changed since then. There were many more houses, and numerous shops had come and gone. There were traffic lights now, which were nice when I needed to cross. All the buildings were formed tightly together, all as if they were of one building, taking up a minimum amount of space, but all had their own character. There was an old church up on the hill with a grey tower reaching into the air with an old, frail cross perching on the top. That was my wife's second home.

Yet, this route was always safe to me. I never encountered trouble before, but ice could be as dangerous as anything with one wrong step, and a slip on the ice, it was just that, devastating. I felt my breath leave when I hit the ground. The thud sickened me and my body went rigid and tight almost immediately. I literally was unable to do anything. Racer then reacted and started barking, standing over me protectively. My lunch was all over the ground.

It wasn't really anything but the fall that struck me. I couldn't move. I couldn't do anything but sit there. I struggled to get my breath back and calm the beating of my heart. One of my ears hit the concrete as was currently throbbing painfully. I sucked in some breath and I tried sitting up, but my body had gone as stiff as if I was dead. For a moment, I thought that I was too pathetic to be alive. This was sad, I thought, almost angry enough to laugh at myself. I was furious that I couldn't do anything. Damn it, I was a Marine when I was younger, I could argue that I still am... but I supposed that a shriveled- up hunk of skin and bone wasn't much of a man, and thus, not much of a Marine.

I was late for a class and that greatly frustrated me. Some kind stranger came over and helped me gather my stuff together. I couldn't stand just yet and the nice man let me borrow his phone. He stood against the wall next to me, his legs crossed, his Oxford shoes tapping each other. They were really nice shoes, expensive, well taken care of with light stitching. I had a pair of shoes just like that in my closet. The ones at home were forty-five years old and a little tight on my feet now, well worn, comfortable. This was a man of distinction, I thought, yet the rest of him was dressed like a soccer-dad. I called my office phone. I didn't lock the door to my office because when the last professor would leave the suite, they would lock the door to the whole group of offices, so as long as someone was there to see that my phone was ringing, I hoped they'd answer it. "Hello?" I heard. "Professor Basilla's office, Dr. Rogers speaking."

"Hello, this is Neal." I said, I just said my name was Neal. Ugh…winded and still trying to catch my breath. "I'm going to be late, something happened. Can you just write on the whiteboard that class is cancelled, if the students could just email me their bibliographies and their outlines, that would be great. If they have a paper copy they can just put it on my desk. I'll try to be in there soon." I could have just stayed home and cried about my dog.

"Are you alright?" he asked.

"Oh, yeah, I'll be fine." I hung up and gave the stranger his phone back. He offered to give me a ride and I took it. He said it was fine I had a dog.

"I have three Labradors back at home, so I'm used to the fur." He smiled and drove me to the college. He talked about how his brother had gone to Hunting's Bridge and that was why he moved to the town in the first place, because he had gotten a job as a janitor here before he got a real job. He said he worked in my building and he recognized me from that. "In '85 were you the one that held the Christmas party? The one in the big lounge?"

"Uh… yes, I think so."

"The one with all the homemade gingerbread cookies and the tea?"

"Yeah, my wife made all that." I laughed, thinking about it.

"You invited me to come when you saw me working the night before. You were there late at like eleven that night. Where you working on a paper or something?"

"I don't know what I was doing."

"You had a dog there, an Australian shepherd, I think, and you said there was going to be a secret Santa and… I… I said that I didn't have money to buy anyone a gift and you said not to worry about it." My heart began to race a bit. "I came the next day in my best clothes and you made some remark about my shoes being shitty," He laughed a bit more. "And you were my secret Santa. You gave me a new pair of shoes. I'm wearing those shoes now." He looked back briefly. "You disappeared so quickly that night I couldn't properly say thank you."

"I guess this is one way of doing it." I smiled a bit.

"I wore these shoes at the job interview at the bank on second street. Now I'm the general manager. The college has let me use my previous employment, as well, to help pay for my son to go there. He's going to be a freshman in the spring. Maybe he'll have you in class."

"Maybe." Or not.

How could anybody possibly recognize me from over twenty years ago? I didn't understand but I was grateful for the help regardless.

When we reached Poplar, I said thank you, he said thank you, and I didn't even risk the stairs but took the elevator. I hated the elevator. I felt lazy. I sat in my chair at my desk and stared at it for a moment. I wasn't actually trembling that bad. I was so sore and stiff from the fall that I was like one big cramp. I hated taking painkillers but I took some ibuprofen hoping that I'd regain movement soon. Dr. Rogers came in and asked what happened. He had been here for about twenty years, that Christmas party in the lounge was his first at the school, and he was a genuinely kind man. He was a bit of an odd fellow though, he was the American history professor and he would ask me a lot of questions because most of the history he taught surrounded the modern era and I lived through a great deal of it and if I didn't, my parents probably did. He wore his hair long, always in a ponytail at the base of his skull. He was blonde and no age could be pegged on him. He taught a course on the Vietnam War many times and I let him borrow some of my memorabilia, including the horrible remnants of my uniform.

I honestly told him what happened on the street and he said, "It's not safe for you to walk here anymore. You need to drive or find a ride, although with your hands and feet acting like they do, I suggest the second option more."

"I know." I said. I hated hearing those words coming from his mouth, coming from anyone's mouth. That walk was my last tie to independence. It wasn't hardly independence though because I needed my dog to come with.

Chapter Nine

Some students came in throughout the day to ask me if they were doing their outline or bibliography right and I was continually impressed by their progress and the good work they were churning out. I felt better after talking to them about their research. It kept me busy enough not to lose my mind.

Racer enjoyed the company, but I knew that while I was here and in-between students coming to talk, I had to pack up some books and some objects. There was only about a month and a half left of school and then I would have to empty out my office completely. I didn't think I'd be able to do it all at once, so decided that it would be better if I did it gradually. I emailed the library director asking if she would take book donations for the school's library and the director said they are always welcome, any books that they already had, would go to the book sale that raised money for a clinic on the other side of town.

I pulled some classics off the shelf first, a few honkers like *Moby Dick* and *War and Peace*, which I only ventured to read once in my life, and anything Ernest Hemingway ever wrote as well, one of which I was still in the process of reading. I stared the books for a moment and put them in the box. My brain was made of these tiny little particles of written word. It seemed so odd to just give them away. I hadn't touched some of the books in many years but... they were still my possessions. I never really was a patron to the library. I'd rather keep the books I read, in case I want to read them later, or keep them on my shelf to look at. It really didn't make any sense when I thought over it... but it was my way of doing things.

Denny came by in the afternoon and said, "So you missed class."

"I did." I replied.

I was lowering some more books into a box. "Before you say you're alright, you don't look all that alright."

"I didn't say I was." I replied honestly.

"What happened?"

"Dog died and ice on the street."

He looked down at my feet where Racer was and said, "But there's one right there."

"I don't know if you were too drunk to notice, but I had two dogs."

"I probably was; I don't remember a whole lot. Sorry."

"No, no, you deserved to blow off some steam." I replied. "While you are here you might as well make yourself useful. If you see any books you want on these shelves, take them."

"Why?" he asked.

"I need to downsize." I said. "I'm going to take them to the library."

"Um, ok." he said.

"So since you are from England, maybe you would

like the legend behind the conquering of England by the Danes?" I lifted up a stack of Viking sagas, *The Pattr of Ragnars Sonnum* and Saxo Grammaticus's *History of the Danes.* He took them and looked over them.

"There's a legend behind it?"

"Made just as a better explanation of the atrocities done to England because I suppose it was better than the truth. Blamed it all on this man, King Aella, and his killing of one Viking, Ragnar Lodbrokr, and his sons coming to get revenge and thus conquering England. It didn't really happen that way, but they're a good read, entertaining really. It's kind of funny when they start talking about killing magic cows with human slingshots."

"Is this supposed to make me think they are more than pillaging marauders?" he asked and laughing.

"It probably will make it worse to be completely honest since it's full of infidelity, because no one in there seems to keep his pants zipped no matter which lady they are with… and then there is a lot of war, people getting skewered, blood-eagled, and full stuff like that. Like I said, there are magical man-eating cows that Ivarr kills, some guy, who is real, but in here he doesn't have working legs, he is one of the brothers that conquers England, the leader. Well, we think. We don't know."

"Uh… that's weird." He paused. "Those books you lent to me at the beginning of the semester, where are they?"

"Top shelf." I pointed. Then I actually looked at him rather than at the books in front of me. "What the hell did you do to your hair?" I asked.

"I cut it." he said.

"Yourself?"

"No." he said with a laugh, pulling the stepstool to the shelf. His hair was in an oddly poufy black cottony ball on the top of his head and he had a half-shaved chin. It didn't make any sense and looked horrid.

"Fix it, please fix it." I said, looking away.

"My sister says it's adorable." he replied staunchly.

"There comes a time when adorable doesn't work anymore. You gotta grow up. Once you hit seventy or so you can be as adorable as you want, until then, please fix that thing on your head and do something with the facial hair. It either needs to have a purpose there or don't have it at all."

He touched his chin and pulled down the books. "Fine, I'll fix it." He paused again and put the books into his bag and pulled out a loose, knit, blue hat. "Now I feel like I have to wear this on my head."

"Did you make that hat?" I asked.

"No…" he mumbled. "My…friend made it."

"What kind of friend?" I asked.

He blushed again and smiled a bit. "A friend that's a girl." I put my head to the side and took in a deep breath. "Fine… my girlfriend."

"What does she think of this haircut?"

"She hasn't seen it yet."

"Just fix it." I shook my head. "She'll thank me."

"Fine, fine, I will." he sighed and laughed a bit.

"Thank you." I said. "Hey, at least you know I'm honest."

"Yes." he said. "So what happened that made you late today?"

"Nothing bad, just took a nasty fall."

"I don't think it's safe for you to walk here." he said staunchly, zipping his backpack up.

"You're not the first person to tell me that, Denny." I said and sighed. "I know that, but I can't drive. That's not very safe either."

"Well, I can. I can give you a ride." he said calmly, looking at the bookshelf again.

"I couldn't ask you to do that."

"You're not. I'm offering." he said. "It's the least I can do for that like seventy-dollar wine."

I shook my head and took a breath. "It was sixty dollars... Denny..."

"Dr. Neal..." he answered back in the same voice.

"Alright." I said. "But I hope you don't mind dog fur in your car."

"You'll be bringing your dog?"

"Yeah." I answered back. He was still smiling, still trying to adjust the hat on his head.

"My sister is going to be so sad that I cut my hair shorter. She was sad that I cut it at all." He looked behind him and said, "I saw something on this shelf, give me a second while I grab it." He searched for a little while before grabbing a book. "So do you like Vermeer? You have a book about him."

"I don't dislike his work." I replied.

"Come on Dr. Neal. He's a good artist. He's Dutch, do you hate the Dutch too?"

"The Dutch people in America, yes, but I have nothing against the Dutch themselves. I don't understand Calvinism though."

"Oh Dr. Neal… well, Vermeer's work: it's colorful, it's bright. Good right?"

"Sure. Not sure why you'd think I like bright and colorful, but it's simple. I like simple. Although he seems to be obsessed with pearl jewelry, pregnant women, and windows on the left-hand side and checkered floors." I said. "It's the same thing over and over again."

"If it works, why fix it? Every artist has things they focus on. It's their signature thing." He took in a deep breath. I could almost see the desperation on him for how much he wanted me to like something artsy.

"It's very nice." I said.

"Really?" He smiled. I didn't reply. "You're lying… dammit. I need to find something you'll like eventually, and I will. I will, I will."

Denny drove me back to the house that afternoon, hat still on his head, but his hair was cut to a reasonable length and he explained to me the entire drive how odd the hairdresser acted when he came back just a day later saying it needed to be 'fixed'. "The poor lady thought that I was making a complaint. I had to explain to her that it wasn't me that didn't like it."

"Well it wasn't a…demand." I pressed, holding tightly onto my leather bag.

"Yes, but I was going to hear about it if I didn't get it cut more, correct?" he asked.

"True."

"So for my own sake and sanity, I cut it." he said. "Although my face is staying the way it is. I don't want to crush my sister too much."

"Of course." I'm not sure how getting rid of confusing facial hair would crush the poor girl, but I wasn't going to argue.

Chapter Ten

The house was odd without Titan in it. It was odd that I wasn't walking in the morning. I didn't feel right without those two things. I was conflicted and aggravated whenever I was home, not that it was a new feeling, it was just growing. I was so confused that I'm pretty sure insanity was not far away. I didn't know how Denny did it, but I didn't feel like this when I talked to him. I actually had a friend.

I tried to clean my dishes in the sink on Saturday morning. I wanted to feel like I had some autonomy left. I listened to the radio; I tried listening to the more modern station to see what I could learn. I was just getting a lot of depressing music, awkward rap songs and a lot of inferences to sex, but not a lot else. I missed my oldies channel, but told myself that I could better myself by listening to this. Yet the kids I knew who were listening to this junk weren't exactly 'smart.' I imagined the people who hung outside of McDonald's smoking pot… and basically all the visuals that had been mostly destroyed in my mind from any homecoming dances I was forced to chaperone rushed back into my brain.

There was some water on the tile of my kitchen floor, flung there in the process of washing dishes. I tried to clean it up but found myself stuck, again. My body's stiffness caused me to slip and fall. Once I landed on the ground, I couldn't regain control. This damn disease, Parkinson's, did its best to destroy me in every way it could. It fought my autonomy tooth and nail. I was left furious and began screaming at the top of my lungs and then I just lay there and cried. It'd been so long since I allowed myself to release all that hate and anger. "I don't know who you are but why are you doing this to me?" I may have been speaking to God. I really wasn't sure what or who I was talking to, if anything. I used to believe in God when I was young. I had a child's faith. But after what I saw in Vietnam, I decided God was impossible. Such things couldn't happen if there was something benevolent controlling the world. Nothing good came from my being in Vietnam, nothing. I lost any sense of belief in anything at all, I didn't believe in the goodness of humanity, in God, in redemption, and after my son died in the Gulf War, anything I believed was confirmed… that war he was in, I didn't know if it ever really ended formally or if what the US was doing right now was an extension of that. My son didn't die for a good reason. His sacrifice had no purpose. I begged him not to go into the military. I didn't want to risk losing him. It was his decision, though, he just said he was going and was hoping to make me proud, even if it killed him in the process. It blew him to bits. I'm not even sure he came home in one piece. I never saw his body. I refused.

Benjamin and I didn't speak to one another after that-from the day he entered the military until he died. He talked to his mother, though, and Tess told me what was going on... but that didn't fix it. It didn't fix anything. Nothing was the same after he died. It wasn't acceptable, the situation Tess and I were in, but we learned to plow through it... well she learned to get through it, I just followed her example.

Her birthday was a week from this day. I dreaded it. It would be the second birthday without her here. In this empty house. This painfully silent, vacant house. I couldn't believe how much I missed both of them, or how painful and terrifying grief was. Everyone I ever loved was gone. Every single damn person was gone. It was obvious that my parents wouldn't be here at this age, but my brother, all of my friends; military and otherwise. A great deal of the former ended up blowing their heads off. I didn't know if it was out of guilt or depression or what. I truly wasn't that old, but it was still a curse to make it this long. It was even more of a curse that soon I wouldn't even have my professorship left to keep me occupied. I was terrified for the time in between the end of the semester and whatever it was that would come afterwards. I really wished I knew. I really wished I could have faith enough to at least act like I knew.

I shoved myself against the cupboard and sat there, to at least keep me in an upright position like a human being. The dog paced around me, whimpering. I didn't know if it was because he was worried or if it was because it was after his normal supper time.

Right then, if I closed my eyes, I saw Vietnam. I could see the dead, the dying, those wounded and thrown on others backs through the jungle. I could smell the humidity, the sweat, the dirt, the blood. I could feel my own fear grow, dragging itself through my veins. I could see children screaming and crying. Their parents begging for something, but we didn't know what, and our orders weren't to listen to the begging and the pleading. We tried not to question our orders. We tried not to look upon the damned as human beings, although they were human. Some people tried to convince us that they were just Nam, nothing more, but it didn't work that way.

I constantly wondered if there was a God and if that God counted the blood spilled by our hands during the war. I didn't know what I thought about that. I did what I did, whether under orders or not. I read that many a Nazi said they only killed those people because they were under orders and they were still deemed evil. I wondered why Americans got a free pass when it came to such things. I didn't see us as any better. I had to see it even though civilians didn't. They ignored those images like they were the plague. Like it would infect them like it infected so many of us.

I had to live with it for the rest of my life and here I was, so many years later, thinking of it, crying out of terror for what I did to others and out of what I saw. I was in a state of panic gripping the very core of my body. I figured I was fortunate to come home in one piece, or to come home at all. The faces of the young men around me, the innocent people who would be hardened at the very least, or killed.

All I wanted in life was to go straight into college but somehow I ended up in an ungodly humid jungle being shot at. I wanted to dive into my studies, get lost in them, to ignore the politics around me. I wasn't part of the peace or war movement. I was just put in the war. I had to fight next to people who also didn't want to be there, and those who originally did, but quickly changed their mind. What they were given was not the glamour they had been trained to think through the Captain America comics, the glory and the valor; this was dirt and grime and pain and death. This was reality, not colorful cartoons of a man who rose from such small beginnings to destroy Hydra. We weren't destroying Hydra; we didn't know what we were really supposed to be destroying at all.

I dug into my pocket. I carried a lighter around all day. This was my buddy Johnny's lighter. He didn't want to be in Vietnam, but ended up there regardless as well. It said, "The unwilling trained by the unskilled to do the impossible for the ungrateful." He'd been blown to smithereens not even a year after he got me free of the Cong. He was too scared to go home, so he stayed for a second tour. He didn't think he'd make it in civilian life, decided to stay until something killed him so he didn't have to do it to himself. Suicide was a sin after all. But so was murder.

I had dozens of lighters, but only of those belonging to people who died. We made a pact that I would take all the lighters from the dead, and then we had a succession line going after that, so they would all be held together in one neat collection forever, virtually at least. It was a compulsion to have one on me at all times, for safety.

I stood up and forced myself to go look at them in a sad attempt of calming myself down. Big Jim's read: "When I die, bury me face down so the whole world can kiss my sorry ass." That seemed to be something I'd be ok with currently.

Our unit wasn't the only one in this collection. Other units gave me their dead's lighters. I received them in the mail up to three years ago, when they stopped. Even when people died of old age, I'd get them, but I knew the difference. I could tell the intelligent and the hopeful apart, those who didn't give a damn, and those that never would. "When the power of love overcomes the love of power only then will there be a chance for peace." There was a Zippo lighter that had a hole blown through it. There was no bullet left in it, but the man lived. The lighter saved him. He walked around with that lighter in his pocket for the next twenty years, and then his wife sent it to me because he had written on a piece of paper my name and address and it said 'send lighter when I die to Neal Basilla." Some lighters had Bible verses on them, especially Psalm 23, I had ten Psalm 23's. "Yea though I walk through the valley of the shadow of death I will fear no evil for I am the evilest son of a bitch in the valley." And my favorite of all made so much sense than anything else: "Being in the army is like using a rubber, it gives you the feeling of security while you're getting fucked." I put, "we're all going to hell anyway" in my pocket as well, the one by my heart in case I ever was to get shot.

I went to my old photo albums; they'd been covered by dust. Tess looked at them shortly before she passed, but I hadn't since. I knew it would hurt too much. Already in pain, I doubted a little more would do much more to me. I opened the earliest one I owned, the photos were black and white. I saw a photo of a young, strapping man inbetween two adults. It was me at the age of seventeen. I graduated from high school and applied to college and was ready to move on with my life. My parents Jenny and Rob were standing on either side of me, wearing similar factory uniforms, light blue denim button up shirts and pants to match. We were all smiling. Very soon after that I was in a uniform. The Marines said they'd pay for my school. I saved up money to go, but not nearly enough, and thought I could do it on my own, but school was expensive. I needed assurance. Most of the pictures following that were of me and some of my buddies in Vietnam. Most were dead by now, either over there, or just because they got old. Some, though, blew their brains out like I wanted to at that moment in time.

Then Tess showed up. I remembered coming back from Vietnam, ready to get through college and move on with my life. Tess was studying in America because she was interested in the whole "hippy" lifestyle. She was one of those free spirits who didn't seem to have a care in the world. I met her at the coffee shop at the University of Iowa. Her hair was long, down to the middle of her back, she always wore something with flowers on it and long flowing skirts (her style never changed). She was always so perky and happy, and my demeanor was very similar to the state it was now. I was a bitter young man. I hadn't recovered well from Vietnam; the shrink said I had shell-shock, and that I had to be a man and get over it. It was a few years still before they realized PTSD was a thing. I just thought I was crazy, or a coward, something like that.

Tess, though, was the most beautiful human being I'd ever seen, inside and out. Her excitement for life and vitality was almost disturbing to me at first but we started to go on dates and I accepted it and even relied on it because I was unable to produce that on my own. I was old-fashioned in every respect. I wore suits, and hats and wanted to go on proper dates like at restaurants and such. She wanted to go dancing, skating, picnicking, fishing, swimming. She forced me to overcome my fears and apprehensions. Within seven months we were engaged to be married. I wasn't able to function without her at that point. I was only alive because of her.

She was so different than I that I didn't know if marriage would really work. We were engaged for almost two years before we actually got married. My parents didn't want me to wait any longer than I already had, but both Tess and I wanted to focus on our school work. Tess was studying to be a nurse, as there weren't too many other options available to her and she was already stuck doing secretary work. I felt like that was snuffing out her light, secretary work, she liked being around people and taking care of them. She was a people person.

While she was still in the United States for school, we got married. Then almost immediately after, I went to grad school for my master's degree at the University of York. We came back to the U.S. upon completion of my master's degree. In the next few years, I received my doctorate. Peace didn't last long of course, my parents died in a car crash a week after graduation. I figured that there wasn't enough left for me in my hometown in Iowa to stay.

I didn't take their death well, as it seems to be the trend. Of course, I was a child to two working parents in a tiny little cracker-box WWII era house. We had no money and that bonded us together. My parents were what kept me going, kept me wanting to achieve more and more. They wanted me to go on to get my doctorate, and they wanted me to be a professional, something they didn't have the opportunity to do. So I went on and did that.

Tess and I moved into this house when she started work at the hospital. The work tired her out, but she found it so rewarding that it really didn't matter. She still took me out dancing, bowling, and skating. We were still young. Yet after I received news of my professorship at Hunting's Bridge College, Tess told me she was pregnant. She was so ecstatic that she made an entire yellow cake with fudge frosting and we ate it all before going dancing again. As happy of a person she was, I didn't think she could get any happier until that day.

The house was put in perfect order. Our child was going to have their own room and Tess spent the whole pregnancy making the house baby-friendly. When Benjamin came, all was perfect in my life and in hers. He wasn't a fussy baby, or annoying, in fact he was pretty independent from day one, as independent as he could be. Tess wanted to give him all the liberty in the world. She told me that a child had the entire universe in front of them and could become absolutely anything that they wanted to be. Endless possibilities. Even outer space was open up to them. That very idea terrified me and amazed me all at the same time and all I wanted was to give him those options. So I worked and produced papers, and published and did presentations and saved up as much money as I could for his future.

Benjamin was a very interesting child. He had phases of interest though; when he was very little it was bugs, then it was plants, so he started working in the garden; then he liked animals, and then he liked science. He stayed liking science. Neither me nor Tess were very smart when it came to science and so what he learned, he learned separate from us, although in the evening at dinner time he would normally tell us what he learned that day. He was a sponge. I was so incredibly proud of that fact. My son was going to be extremely intelligent, he already was at that point.

We would go on walks together when it was nice, Tess, Benjamin and I. Tess quieted just a bit at this point, from reality and age probably. Yet when Benjamin got older and was going to elementary school, which was next to Hunting's Bridge, I would walk with him to his school before going to mine. But Benjamin didn't stay young forever. He grew up just like any kid is supposed to. He took up sports, and kept planning for his future. First, he wanted to be a chemist. Eventually he decided on being a doctor, preferably an oncologist. He liked complexity and how things worked and he liked challenges. I taught my son all I needed him to know: how to work hard. He got a car by the time he was eighteen and was driving back and forth from school. He was gone a great deal of time, but we still had family dinner a few times a week.

It was at one of those family dinners he told me he was going into the military. "Why would you need to do that?" I asked him.

He sat across from me during dinner. We had hot dinner rolls, mashed potatoes and roast beef that night. I could still smell it. He was poking nervously at the meat. "What do you mean, Dad? You were in the Marines, and you said it made you proud to serve your country in a time of need."

"It wasn't a time of need and I wasn't proud." I stated strongly. "You know that. I don't know where you got that idea. There was no reason for that war, and there was no reason for me to do the things I did."

"Dad, things are different now."

"Things are not different." I snapped. "There is no purpose for the war now either. It's not your job to go and fight."

"It's someone's job, and it's my decision Dad." he said. Tess looked down to her potatoes, she was detached, nervous, but she wasn't about to say anything. She decided that her son needed to make all choices for himself.

"It's your life I suppose. If you want to get yourself blown to bits that's your choice, but you have your family to consider." I said.

"Dad!"

"Neal…"

"Do you not know how many of my friends I saw die over in Vietnam? War still kills people, and you are not invincible Benjamin! I don't want you to get killed!"

"Dad, I'm enlisting." he said. "And that's the last I'm saying on it."

Tess and I hadn't talked for days after that. I was so angry. I thought Benjamin was being stupid, possibly throwing his life away for a war that wasn't his problem. He left soon for training. According to Tess, he didn't want to waste any time. He wanted to get his time in.

I was at work the day he left and never saw him again. Tess lightened up after he left, but she spoke to him through letters and the telephone whenever she could. I still had his last letter but I couldn't hardly look at it. I knew what it said. I read it after we received news of his death almost a hundred times until I memorized it. Yet I couldn't remember his funeral. I was in some odd daze of confusion and hatred for everything. I remembered that there was a flag given to Tess that was still on my mantel and that it was a proper military funeral. I thought that if Ben had to die for the country, they owed him a proper burial and respect.

Dear Mom,

Please disregard my previous letter. I don't want you to remember me like that in case something happens. As honest as it was, please just get rid of it. I know back at home it is spring. There will be buds on the trees, and there will be birds in the air. The snow will be gone and the ice. It'll be nice outside. I hope you've started my garden so it can still produce food. Is Annie by the fireplace at night still? Are there cookies in the jar?

The letter ended there. They sent it to us although it appears not to have been finished. There was blood on it, it was in his pocket, taped back together by one of his comrades who thought that we should be able to see it. I wanted to burn it, but it was my son's blood. It was physical evidence he existed, when so much time passed I thought he was just a dream, and his death was just a nightmare.

That letter that Tess was supposed to get rid of was sitting right next to it, neatly folded in its envelope. It was postmarked just a few days before his death.

Dear Mom,

I didn't know that I could feel this way. People are dying and I know that people die, that's normal, but for people to go like this... I don't think there's all that much dignity to it. I don't think I can hear one more bullet going by without losing my mind. Loud noises mess with me. We've lost about three men now. I suppose that doesn't sound like a lot, but it's a lot to me. Something happened to my leg, but I don't know what. It only hurts sometimes, because there are times when I can't feel it, I can't feel anything. Right now, writing this letter I don't feel my hand, and I don't feel the rest of me. I know that might sound bad, but I guess it's for the best. The men around me say that is a good thing, means I'm getting used to all of this. Mom, I don't want to be used to it. I'm tired. Maybe Dad was right, this wasn't the best idea. I went in with the best of intentions, and they are supposed to get you ready for this kind of thing, but nothing does. Nothing. They didn't tell me how I would feel. I know I'm not supposed to feel anything though. I'm a person, though, not a robot. I wish I was a robot, it would make things a hell of a lot easier. I wish I didn't have to send you letters through MRE boxes. This is the first good piece of paper I've seen in a while. I know these things are sort of all over the place, but I don't have any paper left, no one does. It's a miracle that letters can get sent out here, and delivered. One of my friends, he reminds me of Dad, he's really smart and he likes poetry. He brought this book and there is this poem I've been carrying around from him. It's probably not the best poem in the world to keep me happy about the situation, but I've never understood something more in my life. I want you to read it. I don't have a title, but I have the author's name: Edgar Guest.

It is coming time for planting in that little patch of ground where the lad made merry as he followed me around. Now the sun is getting higher and the skies above are blue and I'm hungry for the garden and I wish the war was thru. But it's tramp, tramp, tramp, and it's never look behind, and when you see a stranger's kid pretend that you are blind. The spring is coming back again, the birds begin to mate. The skies are full of kindness, but the world is full of hate. And it is I that should be bending now in peace above the soil with laughing eyes and little hands about to bless the toil. But it's fight, fight, fight, and it's charge at double quick, a soldier thinking thoughts of home is one more soldier sick.

I put the letter away. What I experienced in Vietnam I never wanted him to know, but he had. He knew the same pain I did and probably the same fear, hatred, and anger. It was the worst feeling I ever knew and he died with it in his breast still. He didn't get to see home again. He didn't get to bend above the soil in his garden and just be safe. He died not feeling safe, and that was the worst thing a father could know. I honestly didn't see the glory in him dying for his country if he didn't feel it when he went down.

I looked at his flag. I put the photo albums away, as I cried too many tears in one day. I looked around me and affirmed the fact that they were gone, and they weren't coming back. I just wanted to join them.

Chapter Eleven

The next morning, I woke up early. I was having trouble sleeping. I wasn't comfortable, my entire body felt like there were little insects inside trying to bite their way out. My legs kept moving all night. I hadn't had this problem since I was young, but it came back with a vengeance. I couldn't pace like I did when I was younger. It was about four in the morning. I got dressed while my limbs were comparably calm and managed to climb upstairs. I hadn't been up there in a long while. There wasn't much up there, just one room and a bathroom. That room was Benjamin's. My climbing was more like crawling, as I was on my hands and knees. I took a break at the landing. The carpet felt cold, and the air smelled stale. The door to his room was made of glass and it hadn't been cleaned in a long while. I stood up and walked inside his room. It was as normal as any dead child's room was. It looked untouched from the last time he'd been in it. His pictures were on the wall still, oddly dated from the nineties.

I sat on his bed. The quilt was blue and grey made by Tess, it was as crude as her abilities, but well loved. It was so cold, crisp, and flat as it had lay there for so long. I laid back and stared at the ceiling. There were those "little glow in the dark space" stickers on the ceiling, but having not seen much light in over two decades they didn't glow anymore. I could remember Ben's voice, his laugh. There were books on his shelf that ranged from dinosaur encyclopedias to how-to gardening and then school textbooks that detailed chemistry, physics and medicine, things that I didn't understand. Tess and I decided that our son surpassed our knowledge, and one day he would be something great. I realized neither of us really thought about him dying before us. The world had just grown so safe that people assume that their children will outlive them... if it wasn't for his want to be something great, in his mind, then he would still be alive. He probably would have gotten married, had children. He would have his own house, a career, and he would have been able to do that with his faith still intact.

I fell asleep on his bed, and woke up to my alarm on my watch. It was my backup alarm. I slid back downstairs as carefully as I could before sitting down for some coffee. I had the lighter in my pocket, I felt it with my fingers. It was still cold somehow. I put it on the table and read the words over and over again "We're all going to hell anyways."

Denny arrived on time so we could carpool to HBC. I still had the Zippo in my pocket. "Hi Dr. Neal, do you mind if we pick up my sister from the hospital this afternoon?"

"Um, sure."

"I want you to meet her." he said. I took the lighter out of my pocket and twirled it around my fingers. I'd been to hell and back by the time I was Denny's age. I killed people by the time I was his age, destroyed homes... destroyed livelihoods... destroyed my own conscience. Denny would never feel that desperation. "So what's got you so down, Dr. Neal?" he asked.

We stopped at a stop light and he looked at the lighter and read the words. In response he said, "I sure hope not. I was banking on going the other direction."

"Good." I replied. It's always a good thing he could think so positively, even if I couldn't. I wondered what I was going to do with these lighters...I wasn't going to live forever and hopefully not for much longer. I didn't think Denny would understand them. He lived such a cushy life.

I almost dreaded meeting his sister that afternoon. I was worried that I would break all my wife's rules about how to treat a dying person: #1: don't treat them like they are a dying person, #2: don't treat them like a dying person... so on and so forth. No looks of pity allowed, no change in how you would treat anyone else. The person you are speaking to is perfectly aware of their condition. Denny mentioned that her cervical cancer was stage four now. She probably wasn't going to pull through this. So, she was a dying girl... or nothing but a girl. Denny was maybe 22, making her probably 23. She was too young to die. Correction, she was too young to be this sick. But I knew that wasn't the case. Young people get sick, and young people die.

Yet I still found myself walking through those automatic doors into the hospital, smelling that familiar sterile yet extremely sickly smell that was a hospital. I recognized almost every chair. We were in the oncology wing; my wife had been here plenty. I knew where they did all the procedures. I probably knew a great many of the nurses and doctors as well. The waiting room was just the same as the last time I'd been here, and the last time I was here was the day my wife died. Tess was stubborn, she didn't die until I left the room to get a glass of water because she told me weeks earlier that she didn't want anyone in the room when she finally let herself go. Well, I hadn't left her side a lot that week she was in the hospital; she was too sick for them to move her into hospice at the last minute, so they let her stay. I got the water I wanted and came back and there she was, dead. She suffered so long, lost herself so many weeks before that. I had already dealt with the initial stages of grief. Maybe I just wanted to watch her breathing as long as I could, even if she wasn't there anymore. That cancer was cruel to her, it whittled her away, left her a hollow shell that was only in pain, trapping what remnants of the woman it once contained within it.

Denny knew this wing well enough too. He went straight to the room where his sister was without hesitation. She sat on the bed, looking at her phone. She was in a coat with a hat on her head and sneakers on her feet. I felt like I was intruding. "Henry Helling, there you are." she said. "You said you'd be here twenty minutes ago."

"Sorry, Bridget." he replied. "This is Dr. Neal, and Dr. Neal, this is Bridget."

"Hello, it is nice to meet you." I said. I looked at Denny. "Henry?"

"That's my name." he said.

Bridget laughed and said, "It's really odd. I'm the only one that still calls him that, even though he was only called

Denny because I couldn't pronounce Henry until I was like four."

"Henry?" I laughed again. The name didn't fit him.

"Yep, but please call me Denny. It's even weird when she calls me Henry."

"But that's your name," Bridget said. "I'm still going to call you that, if I don't, no one will." This girl was as thin as a rail, trying to cover up her fragile frame with a bulky blue sweater. Her legs were just twigs and her hands were just bone. Her face was long and round, but her eyes looked like they were massive colored plates that changed in every lighting we were in. I wasn't sure what color they were supposed to be, maybe like a hazel-green, but in some light they were dark brown.

It was interesting to hear the two talk. It was clear Bridget was in good spirits, although her walking was as slow as mine. Denny walked calmly alongside us. The truth of why they were sending her home, though, was because they couldn't do a lot more than the chemo and the radiation. The cancer had metastasized and they were fighting it best they could, but she needed to be home, comfortable, with Denny.

Denny and I went to lunch a few days later. It was a regular occurrence now. He kept telling me that I needed to eat more, I was getting too thin. It was true. I wore belts on a daily occasion, and wore some of my son's old clothes since he was much smaller than I. I had some issues swallowing lately, although that seemed to be the least of my worries, it was it coming back out the other end. It was rather embarrassing, all of it. The fact that it was getting hard to breathe was also embarrassing, but more than that- it was annoying. I was woken up at night by my body revolting against me because of a lack of oxygen. I liked my sleep and the fact I wasn't getting enough of it made me furious.

Yet there I sat with some soup. I really was turning back into a child. All I could eat was soft foods because my jaws were not strong enough to chew. "Kids these days…" I muttered out of response to him talking about video games and street crime.

"Yeah," he said and laughed, cutting into some meatloaf. "They are pretty interesting."

"Careless is a better word. No one is careful anymore. I don't know if it's because young people think that they are invincible or what it is." I muttered. Ben thought he was invincible.

"That's probably a common attitude." he said.

I looked back at the car. I didn't know why I was so nervous. The gargoyle from my office was sitting in the back seat. Denny helped me move it into his car so I could take it to the graveyard and put it by the headstone my wife was under. Well, it wasn't like he helped me, he just did the moving. It was Tess's birthday. It was the only present I could give her. I had nothing else. "When it comes to anything: money, school, drinking, sex. People don't know what certain things can do to them. I don't know if it is because no one teaches them or if they just don't care listening to it."

Denny nodded and said, "I think we learn all of that in school. I remember taking economics modules and we learned how to balance check books, do insurance paperwork, start a retirement fund, so on and so forth. We had courses on how to study, if you can believe that." He laughed. "Not that anyone listened to it. No one really talked about drinking, maybe once in health …" He looked up and said, "I'm still sorry for the way I acted at your house." He was laughing nervously. "Just stressed."

"Understandable." I replied.

"And about that last part, we did have plenty of classes on that. Enough that anyone would be completely aware of the consequences of their actions and what it would take to avoid negative things."

"Don't they teach girls that they need to get that vaccine so they don't get HPV? Or to be careful, well do both, so they don't end up sick like your sister."

He went pale for a moment and looked down at his food and swallowed. "What are you saying? That it's my sister's fault she's sick?"

"No, no, it's just one of the most preventable forms of cancer." I replied. "And most girls with cervical cancer had HPV and HPV can be transmitted."

He moved the food around his plate with his fork and took in a deep breath. "I know that already, she knows that already. We all know that already."

"Denny, uh… you still need to be careful." I replied. "I don't want you to have to fight like I had to at your age." Color seemed to come back to his face and he nodded. "Are you angry with me?" I asked.

"No, no, no, I'm not angry." he said and ate some of the meatloaf, then put the mashed potatoes on top of it and squished it down with the fork. "My sister is fully aware of the reason she has cancer, Dr. Neal. I just am…"

"You're protective of her." I said. "I'm sorry. I know you are, and it's your job to be her brother. I'm just saying that you're helping her fight this battle."

"It's not all war."

"Biologically it is." I replied. "You've seen what it's done to her thus far, and it's probably going to get worse before it gets better." If it gets better, I thought.

"Your wife died of cancer, right?" he asked. His voice hadn't risen back up from the tone it fell to yet.

"Yes, she had pancreatic cancer. She had a three percent chance of survival. When she was told that she looked at me and said, 'that's three in one hundred, that's pretty good odds, right? It's better than no chance at all.' I didn't believe her because when I heard that, it sounded like a death sentence. She was a much more faithful woman than I, though, to God, whatever God it was she was faithful to. She was one of those kinds of Unitarian people. She would say that she was Christian because that's what she grew up learning and she went to church every Sunday and Wednesday and accepted that faith, but she didn't think that God lied to people. She thought most major faiths were right. Well, she prayed and she prayed when she was diagnosed. The more she prayed, the sicker she got, but that was just the way the disease worked. It worked quickly. She deteriorated to almost nothing after about five months. She was only really alive for four of those months. When she realized, she wasn't going to get any better, she was fine with it. She said she got to see our son that much sooner, and I would just have to wait."

Denny looked up at me curiously. "You had a son?"

"His name was Benjamin. He was... I think twenty-four when he died, not much older than you. He was in the Gulf War. He... well, he died in the Gulf War." I sighed, and looked down to my bag. "I want to show you something." I lifted my bag onto the table. "Do you remember the lighter I showed you?" I asked.

"Yeah."

"I have a lot more of them. They were given to me by comrades and some other men that I never met who died in Vietnam, and a few who died otherwise." He looked through the lighters.

"Damn, how many do you have?"

"I have yet to count." I replied, sighing.

"I never want to feel this way, ever." he said, holding some of them up to me.

"It's not a good feeling, Denny." I looked him in the eye briefly. I was never very good at eye contact. "Your sister probably feels this way."

"She hasn't told me." he said.

"Is she older than you?" I asked.

"Yes, by a year."

"She's still protective of you. She doesn't want you to know exactly what she's feeling, that's probably too personal. She doesn't want you to experience it." He took in a deep breath and looked down again. "Where are you parents through all of this?" I asked.

"Well, they're at their house. We have an arrangement. They come up for birthdays, we come down for other major holidays, otherwise we are in our respective places."

"Are they not worried for Bridget?" I asked.

"How worried could they possibly be if they sent us away as soon as they could?" he asked, cocking his head to one side. "I really don't know them all that well, to be completely honest. They send checks in the mail sometimes and there is a twice monthly phone call, but that's about it."

"Are they going to pay for your graduate school?" I asked.

He pushed his half-eaten plate to the side. "Oh no, they didn't want me to be anything but a doctor or a lawyer, something prestigious like that. The very idea of me being a musician or theater major made them nauseous. They said it was low for me to do that. They can't stop me from going to school though. I received word that my tuition is paid for by the scholarship, just not the rest of it. I'll have to work that out soon." He sighed and said, "It'll be a pain moving my sister to another town. I'm glad it's not too far away so she can still go to the right doctors and all." He pulled his fingers through his hair before taking a bite out of his thumbnail. "They are barely paying for that. She can't work; I have no time to work outside of my schooling. Once I'm done with my undergrad, I'm going to be taking care of her day and night till something happens whether she gets better or not, and then I'll have to go to grad school. The school said I could work as a teaching assistant and that would pay for my books, and food but just not housing expenses or her medical expenses either."

"You'll make it," I promised. "There's always a way."

"I'm hoping so." he answered back with a deep breath. We stood up, paid, and left.

He drove me to the cemetery where he helped me place the gargoyle next to my wife's headstone and then I told him I could walk from here to my house, it was just a block away. I wondered why I hadn't visited more, especially since I lived so close. I didn't particularly like graveyards, even though they weren't at all creepy, in fact they were peaceful. Denny drove away and I sat down beside the headstone with my name on it and my wife under it. "So I don't know if you can hear me," I said to Tess. "But it's nice to have something to look at while I talk to you. I brought that goddamned gargoyle. You liked it, well, you can have it next to you for eternity. I'm sure I'll be right there next to you soon enough. I don't think that's much of a bad idea anymore. I wish you could tell me what actually happens. I don't know if I should be afraid that I haven't given my heart to God or something. I'm not saying that there isn't one, in fact there probably is, I just don't know in what form or manner or how to deal with that entity... I'm confused." I sat down next to her name Tess Clarrie Basilla, written in the good sized, light colored granite. There was a little cherub hanging above her name, holding a wreath. Benjamin was right next to her with a smaller headstone, almost completely grey stone, smooth, with his name in manly lettering 'Benjamin Henry Basilla', and I realized why I was so shocked when Denny's name was Henry. That was my boy's middle name, and Tess's father's name, and Tess's great grandfather's name. Tess proposed that it be Benjamin's first name, but I argued that I was too American for him to end up with such a stereotypical English name, and so she chose something from the Bible. I didn't remember, at the moment, how or where the name showed up, but it sounded good enough. She won in both cases, really. My idea was to name him Samuel, but really just call him Sam, like Samwise from *The Lord of the Rings*. He was my favorite character and I thought, superstitiously, if we named a kid that, he would maybe get Samwise's traits. He seemed to be like Sam regardless of the name Benjamin, he was intensely kind and loyal to the point of fault. He only got blown up because he was listening to that 'no man left behind' motto; he went back to get his buddy, and ended up joining him. Maybe he ended up like Sam anyways and it was my fault he was dead. I wished for a son just like that and I got one, only for him to be taken from me at the age of 24. No wonder I couldn't understand how there could be a kind God out there.

"Tess, I miss you. It's not the same around the house without you. You're not singing, dancing, jumping around. You always had a smile on your face. I'm beginning to forget it without looking at the pictures… I'm tired, and I'm annoyed. I am turning into a child for the second time. It wasn't fair how you went and now I understand what it's like… I'm losing my body but not my mind. I'm so aware of what is happening to me. I hate this, and I'm scared. What is it like to die, Tess? Can you even hear me?" I paused and said, "Happy birthday, love." I held myself together although all I wanted to do was cry. I gathered up my bag and shuffled back to my house. I called my accountant and said that we needed to meet.

Chapter Twelve

I shuffled around my house, exhausted after just a few steps, falling over here and there. The only problem with stopping to take breaks to sit down was the lack of chairs around my house, and if I managed to sit down on ground, it was a real pain in the ass to get back up. It was worse than that, it was impossible. Racer was helpful, although it tasked both of our patience for me to stand back up to get to an upright chair, but we managed it. He'd follow me around in case I'd fall over. I sat by the front door on a kitchen chair, trying to tie my shoes. I was so angry I could cry when it took twenty minutes before they were properly tied.

Denny knocked on the door. "One second!" I said as I worked on the other foot. The door opened and he stood at the door and greeted Racer.

"Hey Dr. Neal." he said. "Need some help there?"

"No, no, I got it, I got it. Damn I know how to tie my shoes."

"I'm sure you know how to but…"

"Denny." I snapped.

"What's with all the boxes?"

"Like I said, downsizing." I said, trying to tighten the

knot on my shoes. Finally, I put my foot back on the ground and pet the whining dog.

"In what way?"

"I don't need all of these things, I might as well take some of it to the donation center… and because I'm old enough, a museum."

"If you need some help, I can come over and help you with the boxes and stuff."

"You offered." I said. "I'll need it."

"Well, after classes today, I can come over. I just need to pick up Bridget. I don't like leaving her alone too long. She's with her friend right now, but her friend has to leave at two and…"

"It's fine, it's fine." I said and we shuffled towards the car.

"Have you thought about getting a wheelchair?" Denny asked.

"If I can still walk I'm not getting in a damn chair."

"Dr. Neal, I don't think that it is very good for you to walk this far." he said. "What about one of those walker things to help you?"

"No." I said. "I can do it. I'm not that old."

"It doesn't have anything to do with being old."

"I'm not getting a chair or a walker. I have my cane. That makes me look old enough." We left the house and approached the school. I wasn't bringing Racer today. It'd be short enough. We parked in the student parking lot. I hadn't realized how tired I was until I saw how long of a walk it was to Poplar. The tennis courts were in front of us, surprisingly filled with some students who were all sweaty, young, fit, able to bounce around with ease. "Why did you have to park back here?" I asked.

"This is where I always park." Denny replied. "This is where my stickers are for. I can't park anywhere else. It's a green lot only."

I shook my head and pulled out a sticker from my wallet. "Put this on your car. Park behind Poplar." I said and got back in the car. He shook his head and put the sticker on his car.

"Isn't that faculty only parking?"

"Uh huh." I replied and crossed my arms. "And that distance won't give me a heart attack." He pulled out of the tennis court parking lot and back onto the thin, cobblestone road and we bounced past the student housing. There were six dormitories here, all of them looked alike. I figured if I was a student I would get confused on where to live. We had two male-only dorms, two female-only, and then two of both. The two of both were only made coed about twenty years ago. I didn't really like that idea. I had many girls come and complain to me about how uncomfortable it made them to share their bathroom. I never once had a young man come and complain though. That's how boys worked I supposed.

I'd been inside a few of the dorms before, meeting students in the lobbies. Each lobby was different and had varying degrees of formality. One of them was full of very fine furniture and a beautiful fireplace, grand piano. It was wonderful but I thought that I'd ruin it just by stepping on the pristine white carpet. On the other hand there was one that smelled like beer, probably hadn't been thoroughly cleaned in a few decades, had bottles and cans littered around… it was gross, in every sense of the word and was nicknamed the 'Passion pit' for reasons that I could guess but didn't want to find out for myself.

The humanities building, in which I practically lived, was right next to the dormitories and the mess hall. It was one of the most popular places on campus for the students to study past the five story, ancient looking library. The library really wasn't all that old, maybe a hundred years at max but was made in a Gothic style because the president of the college thought, at that time, it would draw in more students because apparently people like either really old or really new looking things. It seems to have worked because I had multiple students come and tell me that they wanted to come here because it looked like Hogwarts. I decided that if anything looked like it belonged in Europe a couple centuries ago, it was the mess hall. It had a tall ceiling and weird, ageless, looking chandeliers that hung down, but had one massive window that let in most of the light needed to see. Yet the whole campus was covered in stone and towers and ivy. The stone was stained, the ivy was evasive and had been there as long as the buildings.

Denny slowed down at the mouth of the parking lot. "You're sure I won't get in trouble parking here?"

"Well there's a sticker on it. That should be the only thing that matters." I said.

"Alright, as long as I don't get in trouble."

"If you get in trouble they will have to deal with me and the administration here never wants to deal with me. I always win." That last part was a lie. If I always won-I would have a job next semester. I realized I wasn't going to be able to do that job, and the college was right... so I understood their reasoning now, but they still should have given me the opportunity.

I smiled and got out of the car after he parked. I shuffled to the door of the building and rode the elevator up.

"Alright I'll see you in a few hours..." Denny yawned and walked off as I sat in the chair of my very empty office. It felt so foreign now that it wasn't covered from floor to ceiling in books. My raven banner was still up, still staring north-west towards what it wished to conquer. The gargoyle wasn't there anymore there was just an old brick holding the door open, borrowed from Dr. Rogers. It wasn't much of a home-like office anymore. This little piece of the college had been mine for forty-three years now looked like it could just be given to someone else so easily. I'd been here for so long... I felt like this was supposed to be permanently mine as if that would be the only thing remaining of me here after I would leave.

I wasn't going to stay much longer than this but the only person I discussed it with was Dr. Rogers, the head of the department, and Dean Carlton. I begged him not to say anything to anyone else, I didn't want some pitiful send off, with the whole world knowing that I was a pathetic dying mess. The dean of faculty didn't need to tell anyone either. It would be better that way if they wouldn't listen to my pleas. I just wanted my retreat to be quiet. At the same time, though, I supposed like any person, I wished that I wouldn't disappear afterwards. At this point I stopped fearing what was going to happen after I died, I figured that worrying about it wasn't going to do me any good or change anything. What did worry me was disappearing completely off the face of the earth like I didn't exist in the first place. I knew in time that I would, but it I created so many things at this school in particular. I created many courses at this school, I wrote many books and articles, I had things locked in the archives, but who would look at them? What was the point? It really was the only thing that scared me, was to disappear, to have lived completely in vain. It wasn't as if I had children to carry on my memory, or my genes. I failed in that case. I had my writing, and that was it… and this office. It was mine for just a little while.

Dr. Rogers came and knocked on my door. "Hi, Neal, you're here early today." Neal. Just Neal. Did I lose my title of doctor?

"Oh yes," I breathed. "My ride needed to be here early."

"Do you have any hint for me of when I need to take over your class?" he asked.

"Next week. I'll get through this week. I just don't think I'll be able to do classes anymore. There's too much that I need to do." I shook my head and rubbed my hands together. Too much stress. Why did the dean have to be right?

Dr. Rogers nodded and said, "Shall do." I pulled out my manila folders and made copies of everything. "Here you are. Look into it now so you are ready for next week. If you can read all the drafts so you can help with the consultation. I will be available through email as long as I can manage. I want them to feel free to contact me, no matter what."

"Good, good, I will go through these and I have your schedule and syllabus yes?"

"I believe so." I nodded. "It should be in there. Thank you, I didn't imagine it would come to this so quickly."

"It is fine, Neal. It is not like we get to pick what happens to us."

"If only." I smiled and shook my head.

I went through my classes that day, feeling my strength wane in not only my body but my voice. I was becoming wispier and quiet. No matter how much I 'yelled', it was still hard to hear. Yet I had things to pass onto my students with just this week to do it. I wanted to press the importance of not only history, but knowledge in general and their education. I figured that for a few days it would be philosophy class. It was this desperation and worry of the loss of knowledge, as if I had lived this long, gained this much knowledge only to keep it to myself. I doubted the reception of my words to my students, as I feared they didn't care enough to process the importance of my words.

Denny came later that day after picking up his sister. I took a small nap with Racer at my feet before I heard the doorbell ring and I thought my heart was going to jump out of my mouth. "Go open the door Racer…" I mumbled. The dog knew how to do it and went and opened the door. Denny walked in with Bridget next to him. She was thinner now, if it was possible. She was still wearing oddly baggy clothing for her size, and a knit hat on her head. I stood up slowly, focusing on straightening different parts of my body as best as possible and walked towards them as best I could, holding onto the wall. "Hello," I said. "It's nice to see you." I led them into the living room. I set Bridget up on the small couch, the only other piece of suitable furniture in my living room and she was given the remote and Denny retrieved wine. Racer walked up to Bridget and curiously smelled her and then lay at her feet.

Denny and I went into the storage room. "What are you doing here?" Denny asked.

"Packing things up either for the donation center or museum. So just help me get things where they need to be and then if you could take them where they need to go… eventually…"

"Alright." He closed the door. "Sorry I had to bring Bridget. She's been having some more problems… but I don't want her alone. She's been having seizures lately. Sometimes up to twenty times a day, although some days not at all…" He began to pull the boxes near the door and I sat down, holding onto my cane. He just showed me an object and put it in one of two piles.

"What have the doctors said?"

"They say it's a tumor in her brain but they have an idea about how to get rid of it. Apparently, there is like… laser surgery and they are going to work on that like next week."

"Is the tumor metastasized cancer than?" I asked.

He shook his head and shrugged, "I wished I knew.

I'm not sure the doctors know to be quite honest until they get a biopsy."

"Is she doing alright though?" I asked.

"She's hanging in there." he replied, holding up an old lamp.

"Donation center." I pointed.

"She's in a lot of pain, but her mind is still in good spirits, she's almost always in good spirits." I could hear Racer barking.

"Denny!" Bridget called. Denny went to the door and Racer was still barking, but then there was this horrible thud. The thud didn't stop really, it just continued, like a giant flopping fish.

"Shit," Denny hissed. I shuffled against the wall towards the living room, holding myself up. Denny knelt by Bridget who was shaking on the floor. Racer moved onto her and helped to hold her in place and Denny held her head in his hands. He watched her closely and there was some slight pain in his eyes but there was also a look of understanding that this happened many times. It became routine, unfortunately. In fact, that was probably the worst part of it, that this didn't surprise him.

Yet I was impressed that Racer knew it was happening and was able to warn her in some respects and now was caring for her. Bridget came out of it, blinked and groaned a bit. Briefly she writhed on the ground before sitting up. Denny lifted her, almost effortlessly and put her in the chair. "My head hurts…" she said, reaching for a glass of wine.

"No, no, no, we need to get some water into you." Denny replied, he took the glass of wine and put it out of her reach. Racer jumped up and ran to the fridge, his tail wagging madly. The dog grabbed the rag attached to the handle of the fridge and opened it as he had seen Titan do many times. He grabbed a bottle, but in his excitement, his teeth went straight through it, the water began spewing out. He was rather shocked by this happening and dropped it on the ground. He put his paw down on the biggest hole, but with that pressure more water proceeded to come out of the other holes, covering the kitchen tile in water. Racer looked confused, looked over to us and went to get another bottle of water which he held much more gently and handed it to Bridget before running back to the kitchen.

The dog pleaded for help and Denny went over and helped to soak up the water. Racer perked up again and ran over to us. I stood up now, holding onto the mantel. Racer came over to me, but his tail was wagging so heavily that he hit my knees, causing them to lose strength, well, what strength they had at that point, and I fell onto the ground. I sat against the wall with my muscles tightening up.

Denny smiled, and he said, "Aw, come over here Racer. You're ok, you're ok." Racer stood up and went over to him and Denny patted his side. "See, you're a good boy."

Bridget smiled and said, "That dog knew it was coming, the seizure."

Denny held Racer near to himself. "Dogs are good that way." He looked over to me and said, "Ok, let's get back to work. There's a lot to do." He held his hand out to me and I took it so I stood back up. We went back into the room we'd been working on. It smelled like old paper and photographs when we walked through the door. There was a pile of them in the corner of the room rotting in folders. Most of the room was separated into three piles: those going to the donation center, the museum, and the things we hadn't gone through yet.

Denny picked up a bundle of old paint brushes. "Whose were these?" he asked.

"They were my wife's." I said. "Tess liked to paint. She's wasn't Caravaggio or anything, but she liked it."

He looked at them and touched the bristles. "How old are they?"

"I don't know, from the eighties probably at max, that's when she started painting."

He smiled and asked, "Can I have them?"

"Do you paint?" I asked.

"No, no, I can't hardly draw stick figures, but Bridget's been into art for a little while. I bought her an easel and some supplies a few months ago. She likes to sit out on the patio and paint."

I nodded and said, "Yeah, you can take them." I paused for a moment and rubbed my hands together. "Why'd did you get her interested in art?"

"She doesn't like being stuck in the house all day, and reading has been giving her headaches, and will until they get that tumor out. The TV and radio give her headaches too because of the high-pitched sound that comes out of them, so I figured that she could paint or something like that. She's no Caravaggio either, but I like her work."

"Wouldn't you say that you are a bit biased?" I asked with a smile.

"Well of course, but now I can have something more

than photographs in case..." he stopped there and went to put the brushes in his bag. "I have some videos of her dancing too."

"There's more supplies in that box over there. I don't know how good they are anymore." I pointed at a box that had a checkmark made with a permanent marker on the side. He went over and opened it up and dug through it. He picked up a stack of crinkled papers.

"Dr. Neal, I think these are Tess's paintings." he said and held one up to me. It was a cat sitting on a window sill looking outside. He sounded like he knew her.

"Yes, yes, I remember her painting that. We had a cat for a good nineteen years, Oscar, that's him. Yes, it's hers."

He smiled and said, "Well what do you want me to do with these then?"

"I don't know." I replied. There was no use keeping them or getting rid of them.

"I think you should hang them up somewhere, so you can see them." I shook my head. I didn't want to see them. I didn't want to think about Tess right now, it wasn't like I needed anything else on my mind. "Dr. Neal... she painted these with the intention of someone looking at them and you have just kept them hidden in this room for a long time. I don't think it's fair to her that you are hiding them."

"I don't care if it is fair or not. She didn't paint them with the intention of anything but having fun and I don't think that a dead woman cares whether or not someone is looking at her artwork. Just put them in a folder and keep them there." I stated strongly and rubbed the back of my head with my hand. Denny just sighed and put them in a folder and placed the folder on a shelf. He calmly walked back to the box with the supplies and searched through it for anything useable. He smiled when he pulled out an old paper Burger King crown.

"Now look at this." He quickly put it together and placed it on his head. The crown was bright yellow with ridiculously flat looking colorful gems.

"Goes with the ridiculous accent." I said.

"Ridiculous? And how long were you married to an English woman?"

"A long time." I replied, smiling just a bit. "But she didn't sound like she belonged on the BBC."

"So why did Tess have this?" he asked. He really sounded like she was familiar to him.

"How would I know? That woman was crazy."

"Crazy in a good way?" he asked.

"Well, of course, but still, you think you'd know how someone's mind works after being married fifty years, but it doesn't work that way. At least not with us. So if you get married, don't act like you have to know everything, it's probably better if you don't really."

"Huh." he said.

"Are you?"

"Am I what?"

"Thinking about getting married."

His eyes bugged out of his head for a moment and he took the crown off immediately. "Huh? What?"

I laughed. "As far as I'm aware you've already slept with her, that's like half of being married."

He shook his head and said, "Uh I don't think that's how it works these days, no, no, no."

"You aren't thinking about marrying her. Ever?" I asked.

He blinked furiously for a moment and bit his lip then put one hand up to his shoulder and one across his stomach, the way he stands whenever he's nervous. "Well I haven't really thought about that…"

"See when I was young, people didn't just date for dating's sake, much less anything else, so…"

"Yeah, times have changed a bit since then." he replied. "Hmm… uh…"

"Yes?" I rose my eyebrows and sat further back on the chair.

"I don't know!" He laughed and bit his lip again. "I haven't thought about it!"

"If you keep doing that you're going to bite it off all the way."

He looked surprised and sat down on the ground, his legs straight out in front of him. "There's too much stuff to do before I get married, Dr. Neal."

"And what would that be?"

"Get through graduate school." he said.

"See I would have gotten married even sooner but when I came back from Vietnam I realized that I was lucky that I didn't lose my head while I was over there. But I suppose that just because there isn't a gun pointed at your head doesn't mean you should wait till you're old."

"What would you consider old?"

"You're already old enough." I replied. He was quiet. "Is she not the right girl?"

"How the hell would I know?" he asked. "I…"

"Well it's not a good thing you're questioning it. Just letting you know."

"Did you not?"

"We were engaged in a few months, I told you." I replied. "Took a while to actually get married though. I just want to say that you need something a bit… happier in your life than hanging around dead people so much."

"Last I checked, you were still breathing."

"And when did you check?" I asked. "It's not like you came over here to make sure that I still have a pulse."

"Well, my assumption is that as long as you are talking that means you are breathing." he replied, his eyebrows raising just slightly. "If we don't keep going with this sorting, it'll never be done. You have too much stuff." Denny smiled and looked at me for a brief moment. For about half an hour we worked in silence until we needed a break. I needed to get a drink of water and Denny just wanted to sit down. Bridget was standing up, holding onto the wall for support. Her eyes were a bit glassy and she was walking to the kitchen.

"What are you doing?" Denny asked her.

"Getting myself a glass of water." she said.

"Go, go, sit down, I can get it."

"No, I can do it myself." she replied. "It's not like I can't." She took a glass from the counter. I no longer kept them in the cupboard because I couldn't lift my arm up that high to get them anymore. They simply wouldn't listen. She filled up the glass at the faucet and drank out of it. I knew she was weak, but was surprised her knees gave way and she fell down; the glass shattered in the same place that the bottle of water leaked earlier.

There was a look of resignation along with terror on Denny's face. If he was a bit more energetic he'd probably say something like 'I told you so.' This wasn't the time though. He ran over to her and picked her up like a child, put her on the chair as he had earlier and cleaned up the mess. "Just listen to me next time, Bridget." he pleaded. "We don't need you getting hurt. I already worry about you enough."

Chapter Thirteen

Denny and Bridget decided to come to my house to make cookies and cake. I offered them my massive kitchen anytime they wanted to use it since they were living in a dinky apartment. The two kids came and Bridget actually hugged me. It was startling how her touch was frail and cold. She was as dead as I was. She was bundled up in a hat, scarf and a very fuzzy sweatshirt and tall maroon stockings on her legs. Denny came in, his hand was on her back and they sat at my table. "Thank God you broke that out." Denny said when he saw the wine sitting on the counter, a good French blend I hadn't even thought of drinking myself. It was one of Tess's favorites.

"It's for the both of you. You can't just suck on the bottle yourself." I said looking at Denny.

"Yes, sir. I think you're giving me a bad drinking habit." he said with a laugh and poured the wine for all three of us. I didn't know how to drink it, though. The trembling in my legs stopped by now, although it left me stooped over badly like a real hunchback and I couldn't stand hardly at all, but my hands were still in bad shape. I supposed that they started me out on the disease and they were going to end it as well. "Dr. Neal, do you want me to put that in a different cup?" he asked.

"Yes, yes, you can put it in one of my travel mugs." I said with a sigh, feeling once again humiliated, but at least it was a common feeling. The kids got to work while I sat at the table. "You should tell us more about this girl." I said.

He turned around and blushed a bit. Bridget answered, "Yes, you should. Who is this mysterious girl you keep blushing and giggling about?"

"Uh…" His nose crinkled and he rubbed his hand against his arm like he did when he got nervous. "Bridget, you know her."

"Oh yes, I probably do, but Dr. Neal doesn't. And you've never said her name." She cocked her head to one side and smiled. "Tell us, tell us," She was poking at his side just like a sister would do.

"Fine, fine, fine." he spit. "Ella. Her name's Ella. She's from the school Bridget went to. She's at the graduate school I'm going to."

"Ella." Bridget smiled and said, "You little twerp." She looked at me and said, "She was in my dancing classes, she was always in my dancing classes…" She paused and then burst out saying, "You know what, when you told me you were going out with her a few months ago… ah I should have seen this coming! I just didn't think it'd last… hah. Seems I was wrong."

Denny looked down to his feet and I said, "So how much do you like this girl?"

"Yeah!" Bridget added. Denny didn't respond.

"I would reckon that you like her a lot from what I've heard." I replied.

"Really?" Bridget said with a very sisterly voice. "Tell me more." Her eyes teased him.

"Dr. Neal." Denny's voice pleaded childishly.

"Shall I tell her?" I asked, sipping some of my wine from the travel mug.

"You should," Bridget answered.

"No, no, no," Denny said. "I like her a lot. Ok? Let's get back to baking."

"I need to meet this girl." I said.

Denny sighed and leaned against the counter. "Why is it such a shock that I have a girlfriend? Really…"

"Cause you're my brother." Bridget answered. "You've never been very good with the ladies."

"I could have guessed that." I added. "That haircut… did you have that bad haircut often, because that would explain a lot."

Denny shook his head and said, "I was never bad with the ladies. I just was too busy to date." His voice was uncomfortable but matter-of-fact.

"That's your excuse." Bridget said. "You're just too shy. That's the problem. If you aren't acting- you can't do it."

"That's not true." Denny defended with an almost whining tone. They were putting the first tray of cookies into the oven. I still called them cookies with all my might to this day despite forty years of hearing the word biscuit by my wife. These were not biscuits… they were cookies. Tess never relented to her vernacular.

"I feel like I should call her." Bridget sat down at the table and pulled out her cell phone. She put it on speaker. After a few rings, someone answered.

"Hello?"

"Hi, Ella, this is Bridget Helling."

"Bridget! I haven't heard from you in a while! It's nice to hear from you!"

"It is nice to talk to you as well. I'm with my brother right now, and he was just telling me about you. We should get together some time, but I think my brother's been avoiding it." Bridget's eyes went to Denny who was rubbing his arms nervously.

"Is he there?" her voice dropped to a disapproving tone.

"Why, yes he is." she said, smirking.

"Denny! Have you really been avoiding us getting together? Really! We are going to talk!" There was a pause. Denny looked like he was going to say something but just looked at the phone, shaking his head and sighing. Bridget wished Ella good luck on her practice, and then looked at Denny.

"Do you try to make everything a problem?" he asked Bridget.

"That's my job as your sister." she said. "Don't let the biscuits burn." I almost wanted to cringe when I heard that word.

"Well I'm going to hear about this later."

"Yes, you are." I added. He smiled and shook his head.

Chapter Fourteen

Resting in my armchair or rusted in my armchair rather, I was sipping at some whiskey. This was a strange occurrence for me, but there was a bottle of Penderyn that had been sitting on my counter for some time now and needed to get, well, drunk, drank, whatever. I hadn't been much of a whiskey drinker since Vietnam. It was this that spiked my memory into thinking it was back in the sixties.

I tried so hard and so long to keep this out of my mind. It was a time in my life that I would be very happy and grateful to forget entirely. Yet I was already cynical before I left, it just affirmed my theories. I stared at the line of lighters Denny put up on my mantelpiece. My arms couldn't raise that high to move them anyways, so there they stared back at me, laughing, mocking, sneering… all those eyes from all those men, all locked right in front of me. Strangely enough, though, my body was calm. I could hold the glass. I swallowed one shot after another, hoping that this ever growing gnawing of pain in my legs and my chest would somehow subside.

It didn't.

It refused, like it was its own living entity.

The first image that came to mind was Johnny Coffer. A young man, nineteen years old, hair grown longer than it should have, a scraggly darkened blonde. He sat on a flat-bottomed fan boat on a river, eyes straight ahead, shirt unbuttoned, his dog tag rusted with a giant .50-calibere gun sitting in front of him. His eyes were locked on nothing in particular, fingers curled over a dead cigarette. River patrol was his job that day. I was with him. Barry Williams was sitting behind me. A long-faced math nerd with glasses the size of his large square nose. He counted his kills. Lance Boleyn, a native of New Orleans with the most difficult Cajun accent I had ever encountered sat with his bare, painfully muscular arms crossed on his knees, eyes keenly staring ahead. He came to prove to the world that black men were men. He had that weird complex about him. I always thought that if the world had seen this man in action, they'd think twice. But the world didn't see him and they didn't particularly care.

The squad leader, Russell Rod was in the boat behind us. He was a man who wore as little on his torso as possible past bullet racks and three necklaces: his reddened dog tag, and a swastika attached to a rainbow peace sign. I never understood him. He was loud mouthed and was the worst chain smoker I'd ever seen past my grandfather. He was with Big Jim Medicine, which really wasn't his name, but we called him that regardless. He was a Navajo who wrote a letter every day to his family, and none of us could read it. His father was a code talker in WWII. He became a code talker during the Cold War. At least he made it.

This all was thought of in perfect clarity, as clear as if I could smell the smoke of Rod's cigarettes wafting over, Bo's stink, and the dead fish rising to the surface of the river. We made camp that night, all of us exhausted but on high alert. There was no fire, just our canteens and some bad food. We were stationed beside a village that was deemed safe previously. Coffer was playing an old guitar. The only songs he knew were the Beatles and the Monkeys, but he never had the energy to sing along. His face was hollow as he did so, lost somewhere else. Bo knew many of the songs and his energy never wavered. He sang and smiled and he just seemed to still grasp the concept of life. I felt gone at this point, my pockets were heavy with lighters and it had only been a year and a half. There was seven months still to go. I was stupid, signed up for two tours to stay with Johnny.

That morning was bright, smelled like smoke and dew. The humidity didn't leave that night and just grew in intensity during the day. I thought I'd never feel dry again. Rod took up a game of baseball with the village children, teaching them how to hit a ball he carried around in his pack with some large sticks. They were laughing and giggling. Bo stood up and joined them. He and Rod were about the same height, same bulk, and they absolutely towered over the children, but they didn't show fear. They were calmer than I was when I met the two. Big Jim was at his letters still, producing page after page after page that I didn't know if it was sent or how. He kept them in plastic baggies to protect from rain because rain liked to ruin everything. Even fire blaster tanks. Fire blaster tanks are useless in a swamp.

We weren't here to sit, but our orders were few and far

between. All of us in Nam felt rather lost. Confused really. We didn't know why we were here or what we were supposed to be doing. So baseball it was. We were always told we needed the non-Vietcong to like us and their new government so the communists couldn't prevail. Communism was evil. Whatever government these Vietnamese were trying to get was good. That's all I knew.

I killed men. Marines were killed. Soldiers were killed. Airmen were killed. I had their lighters. I knew that too.

We started into our patrol of the forest surrounding the village. Rod was in the front as always, tramping along, less cautious than usual, lightened by his game earlier. Bo was on my left, Coffer on my right, Big Jim behind me, Williams to my diagonal. Tromp, tromp, tromp… *and never look behind, and when you see a stranger's kid pretend that you are blind.*

It was so simple, so quick. One step. One large concussive shock. All of us on the ground. All of us running for cover. All of us but Bo. Bo was down. Big Jim and I instinctively wrapped our spindly (in comparison) arms around him and struggled to get him to cover. Coffer ran backwards behind us, covering us. He shot shots, I didn't see where, I didn't see who.

The smoke was thick. The air was hot. My lungs were complaining. Bo was complaining. We took shelter in an abandoned shack made out of reeds and mud. We lay Bo on the ground, Rod right next to him. Both were bleeding, both in shock. The sound of helicopters approached. Big Jim knew Medicine, hence the name, but nothing taught at Harvard. "You ain't gonna do no voodoo are ya?" Rod asked

Big Jim, who just smiled sadly and began yanking off the man's clothes.

Our canteen water went to cleaning wounds. Coffer and Williams stood outside keeping the perimeter. "One!" Williams called. Very subtle, I thought. "Two! Three!" he called with the shots. We were surrounded. With the list of things I still didn't know, was if we were surrounded by live bodies, and he was counting how many he saw, or how many he shot.

Bo seized my hand, curling his fingers so tightly I thought my hand would contort and break. He was a man of words, and in this case he wasn't short of them. He would tease me about my beliefs, him being a Baptist, and I being nothing. "My friend the skeptic sees no truth in man, while I believe all things I rightly can…"

"Bringing poetry into it, this must be bad." I breathed, smiling. "Stop it, right now. You hear me? You do not have permission to-"

"To die?" he asked.

"Exactly."

"You are a Marine, you do not die without permission."

He smiled a bit and shook his head. Blood on the teeth. Not good, not good… I thought. Big Jim pointed outside, "I need a leaf. The small green kind with the spikey sides, slightly blue tint."

"That's specific…" I muttered sarcastically and took up my gun and stepped outside the shack and into the brush.

"Where're you going?" Coffer asked.

"Big Jim wants a leaf." I responded.

As I stepped further I heard, "Cong!"

My heart beat fast. Williams frantically yelled out numbers, but then fell silent. I peered out from behind the tree and tried desperately to see the shack. The amount of silence that had fallen around me dug deep into my skin and my throat.

All went black with a cloth around my face, my throat, my mouth. Yanked behind and slammed onto the ground I was then dragged, my feet unable to grasp the earth. On we went, the men were Cong, I assumed, speaking quick paced gibberish to themselves. Slammed onto the ground once again I sensed all the bodies around me, mostly live.

Curdling breaths, shallow, shaky ones too… Bo. They got Bo. Damn it. Fuck them. Fuck everything.

Dragged again. Door shuts. Cool surface. Arms still tied behind my back. They asked me a question. I couldn't understand the question. I had one thing to say. "Pfc. Neal Basilla 235144." Gun wacked to the head. Again, "Pfc. Neal Basilla 235144." Again. "Pfc. Neal Basilla 235144." If I'm all that useless kill me or leave me be.

A heavy door slammed shut. Silence. Darkness. The thing still on my face made it impossible to take in a good breath. Light, though, then dark… night. I collapsed on the ground of the little shack thing. I couldn't lie down, there was no room. My body was crunched uncomfortably, burning, aching, complaining as much as I wished I could audibly. I began to rub my face against the shack wall, loosening the band around it. Eventually it fell over my neck. I reared my head forward like a horse until it fell off completely. Wishing I was nimble enough to get my arms to the front, I tried, and tried. Morning showed itself, my arms were sore and felt like gelatin.

No food. No water. But it rained the next day. I opened my mouth and let it come through the slits above me. Shrieks ensued. I couldn't hear who they belonged to. The door was yanked open. Thing was tied on my head again. "Pfc. Neal Basilla 235144." I said. Smack, down on the ground. Their voices didn't register in sentences, although it was broken English. There was a high pitched, terrible ringing. My mouth was so dusty, parched. I wanted water more than anything else. "Pfc. Neal Basilla 235144." Again and again and again for who knows how long before the door shut. Following what I did the previous day, I removed the face thing. It took longer and by then the rain had almost completely quit. I got a few drops in. More shrieking. Terrible, terrible shrieking.

That night it was quiet. "Bass." I heard a voice say. The voice was smooth, rounded.

"Big Jim?" I breathed, coughing. "Big Jim!"

"Yep."

"Who else is there?"

"They got Bo." he breathed. "Rod's dead."

"Rod?" I squeaked.

"Spit on them. Something. He's outside on the ground."

"When'd they do it?" I asked.

"I don't know. A while ago. When he stopped talking I guess."

"He talked?"

"No, that's why I know he's dead. There was... that... you know... cut him, all up. Yeah..."

"You talked?"

"No. Act like I don't know English." he answered. "Works." There was small little laugh.

I tried to think of Russell on the ground, his beaded hat and swastika all bloody. Eyes opened, staring, his terrible, and great smirk memorialized on his face, mocking the Cong.

I didn't do so well in a few days. I kept mumbling my ID, hitting against the wall, going in circles, bouncing off the surfaces, rocking back and forth, unable to sleep, unable to focus, or concentrate.

Pfc. Neal Basilla 235144

Pfc. Neal Basilla 235144

I heard nothing more of Big Jim Medicine. Or anyone else. There was just... terrible, horrible, awful, excruciating silence and it was doing nothing more than fucking with my mind. I couldn't even talk, how could the Cong get anything out of me?

No food. Food... water... oh yes, water... air... all I wanted, those things. Or to be lying on red ground with that peace loving Nazi... who was fighting in a communist country... befriending an Indian and a black man... I'm not sure how that man worked. I could laugh now... but that's not what was going through my mind then.

"Bass?" A voice entered my mind. Night. Couldn't see anything, not even stars. "Bass?" Voice spoke again.

The door shook for a second and I jumped back, trying to get away from the impending bonk on the head. I began my tirade.

Pfc. Neal Basilla 235144

Pfc. Neal Basilla 235144

Pfc. Neal Basilla 235144

The door kept shaking until the thick wooden thing splintered and I saw two figures standing straight in front of me. Rounded helmets, stupid glasses, Rod's favorite Hitler Youth hair... Coffer, Williams. They picked me up off the ground and dragged me straight out. I tried to talk only one thing kept coming out of my mouth, "Pfc. Neal Basilla 2351444."

"Well, at least you know who the hell you are you bastard." Coffer said with a laugh.

Sitting at a hospital in Saigon. My ass was nothing but bone. My head was wrapped in bandages and I was sucking down soup and bread. "You eat too fast you'll explode." A patient told me.

Bo and Big Jim Medicine were alive. Sort of. Not really. But they were breathing. Bo was missing an arm. That big concussive blow did some damage. Big Jim wasn't conscious just yet. Had him on a feeding tube, breathing on his own. Thankfully this meant we all got shipped home. I could be "done".

Chapter Fifteen

I relaxed in my office. I wanted to spend some extra time there. I was cleaning out my drawers. That was the last thing I needed to do. I didn't remember the last time I did this. The desk had four sets of drawers, all of varying sizes and shapes. One was immediately under the writing portion of the desk and was shallow. I opened it and saw on the left many old yellow post it notes. I had a habit of always reading with sticky notes. In research books, on papers, all over the white board and office. Yet I didn't know that I had such a large stash stuck in the bottom drawer. There were many old school manuals and random pieces of useless paper that had been stuffed in there in the duration of my stay. I pulled out the old ads and piled them up on my desk. There were some old Christmas cards in the back. I put them in their own pile before finding lost pens and pencils, which I left in the drawer.

I picked up the Christmas cards, they were all from one girl, Sarah. She was one of my best students in all the years of my teaching. She was my advisee, thirty-five years ago. I remembered her first day of school, she immediately came to see me. She was a small, nervous, frail looking girl.

She acted like she was hardly over the age of fourteen. Her hair was a long, grayish blonde in a braid at the back of her head. The first time I saw her she was wearing a skirt and a white cardigan. She sat down on the same chair that still sat in my office and she asked me about signing up for classes, which was routine. Then she began to cry. She was sniffling when she walked in and I knew she was homesick, but soon found out it was more than that. She told me that her parents never wanted her to go to college. They were hoping that she'd stay home, learn to be a housewife, and have that be her occupation. She didn't know what she wanted to do, but she knew that she didn't want to do that. She wanted to go to college because she loved learning. That was all she needed, I told her, the ambition to be something more than the expectations put in front of her. I told her that my own wife was told the same thing, but when she went to school, there were few options put in front of her beyond being a teacher, secretary, or a nurse. Sarah had more options.

I told Sarah that she should take all introductory courses, so she could figure out what she was most interested in. She took entrance speech class, and as I suggested, a religion class (taught by a man who was a close friend of mine who was very liberal thinking, even for the modern time), introductory chemistry, and then my American history class. After two weeks, she came back. She wasn't crying this time, but I could tell she was distressed. Already she was confused about life. She had grown up, obviously, in a very small, isolated world. She had one sister, who was younger than her, and her parents were extremely conservative and had her go to a private Christian school. I didn't think there was anything wrong with that kind of education, but she obviously wasn't taught about the real world. She was shocked by the drinking in the dorms. She was shocked by the presence of men having free range in her dorm as well. Then she was shocked by her classes. Not only during the first two weeks of class the first thing on my to-do list was to set American history right. What she learned as a child was that the founding fathers were perfect Christians, and I wanted to express the truth behind the pilgrims, the founding fathers and the rampant genocide occurring in the US. The land in America wasn't free, there were people living on this land before we were. She learned the truth about how slavery got abolished and the civil rights movement. In her chemistry class, she learned a part of science that she never thought existed. To realize what everything was made of, atoms and all the elements, it shook her faith.

The religion class, was driving her up a wall. It was about the tradition and history behind Christianity and an analysis of the Bible, but she didn't like what she was seeing. She hadn't actually read all of it before, but going book to book, analyzing what was going on, the history and the theological questions were making her uncomfortable. It wasn't all bright, shiny, and straightforward as she thought. Although not a Christin myself, but being the husband of one I told her, "I don't think God is that straightforward, Sarah."

I remember her saying that, "But it just seemed that way... up until now... I don't know what to do." I told her that college was a place for her to look at reality, all the knowledge that she could get her hands on, to grow up, to become a woman, to decide what she believes for herself. She came every week for the next four years of her schooling. It didn't seem much like therapy until looking on it now, but I had a Christmas card from her every year since then. Including this year. Ten years after graduating she got married, and she had two kids, but she also had a career. She became a librarian, although it was quieter than I thought she would end up with, it seemed fitting. She had a hunger for knowledge and a love for reading. The knowledge that she craved was in the books and now she had an endless supply and she was surrounded by them.

The cards had an evolution of their own, the years it was hard they were cheap cards, the years it was good there was gold envelopes and velvet, and then after she had kids the cards became those photo cards. She had two girls, and they were cute, they were happy, and the more they grew up, they looked very independent and very successful. When they were little they sent me hand drawn pictures and random trinkets. She had two doctors now. They became what my wife wished to be, but in the time my wife lived, it wasn't possible. Now, just about anything was possible.

Denny knocked on the door as was custom now. It was normal. He sat down on the old chair that so many students sat before him. I was thinking of Sarah briefly, but his smile was oddly calming and my mind cleared. "So how is the book so far?" He told me to read the entire works of Victor Hugo but a few days ago. In my long, boring weekend, I managed to pull through it. The entire brick of it.

"It's done." I replied. "Somehow, I got through it."

He held his hands on his water bottle, and he looked at it briefly. "Well, I'm more confused about humanity now than I was before if that is impressive at all." I smiled a bit, chuckling. He said, "I actually did throw the book at the wall after the ending of the Hunchback. I don't know why I trusted the happy title of the last chapter 'the marriage of Quasimodo' I really thought…"

"You shouldn't have thought." I said.

"Apparently."

"Though Les Mis wasn't really all that miserable of a read. It was long and through a combined effort of both of the books I managed to probably have every street of the early modern Paris painted in my mind… although I don't think anyone really had that eventful of a life."

"People really did fight in the revolution." Denny said.

"It's not during the revolution, Denny… Did you not even read the damn thing?" I almost shrieked. It was more of an exclamation.

"Well, I read it… a really long time ago."

"And when was that?"

"Before I had to be in the musical. I was the boy that got shot the first time." He laughed.

"Ugh…"

"At least they died fighting for something." I didn't like that statement.

"And what were they fighting for? Did they even know?"

"Like all the liberty and equality and stuff." Denny laughed, leaning against the door with his arms crossed.

"How was the full revolution not enough? Right after

that I guess they decided, oh I'm not happy with the results, lets decide to sit here and complain about what we don't like, and decide to fix it by dying. I wonder how that worked. They didn't even know what liberty and equality was. And what was that to a bunch of spoiled, rich, drunk, gay brats?"

"Uh…"

"Well, they were, I read between the lines, or even the more than obvious stuff too. They're French, that's all I have to say."

"Uh, well, next topic I guess. Well, this book doesn't help me understand love." Denny laughed. "In fact it probably makes me more confused."

"It isn't helpful, I don't think it's supposed to be helpful and most of us in the world don't understand it." I sighed.

His face twisted a bit as it usually did during conversations. He sat down in the chair with hands clasped together, in between his knees, although he was slouching just a bit which was a good sign that he wasn't too uncomfortable. If he sat up straight or slouched further, I would have been a bit concerned. "I know what it is."

"Do you?"

"Well, somewhat."

"I can tell you that it doesn't have to be as complicated as it is in these books. As long as the girl you are going after isn't some pretty hippy who is running from execution for witchcraft and you happen to be semi-normal looking, you should be fine. But for me, like with my wife, I met her, we went out, I realized that I saw her in my future and couldn't see my future without her, asked her to marry me and then we got married. It's simple."

"How could it possibly be simple? I'm confused all the time with Ella."

"That's because she's a woman. You'll never understand her. I was with one for fifty years and still couldn't comprehend how her mind worked. Or any woman's mind for that matter. I don't even know if women know how their own minds work."

"Well, Ella did say to me if she acted really weird she couldn't help it because it was hormones." Denny laughed, although at the moment he began to rub his right arm with his left hand and he looked to the door nervously.

"That's true, but it's worse during pregnancy. My wife wanted to eat the weirdest of things… it was like one minute she wanted to eat an entire brick of chocolate, which they do sell by the way, and then the next moment she would get sick of chocolate and want to eat frozen whipped cream which is basically like really cheap ice cream. She ate so many tubs of Cool Whip that she wouldn't eat it for the rest of her life. Benjamin even hated it. Then she'd want to get some fast food, which she never liked before she was pregnant, she thought it was disgusting, but I guess she really wanted to get a lot of fat and salt into her. She was always such a small woman that when she started to get big she couldn't handle it. She'd just stand in front of a mirror laughing and crying at the same time wondering how this little parasite could grow inside of her, come out, as a human being, and her love it. She just kept shrieking 'what is this thing doing to me.' The morning sickness… ahh, and

I thought that was bad. Then menopause hit. The hot flashes... she'd go outside in the winter and stand in the snow. Then the cold flashes, she'd chug down hot water, which is probably not healthy. Then the mood swings... God the mood swings... it was as bad for her as it was for me because she knew it was going on and couldn't do anything about it."

"Cruel thing nature is." Denny said with a laugh. "I can see how that works for my sister growing up. All of a sudden when she was like twelve I couldn't even talk to her without either her crying or going ballistic. I mean she's calmed down since then... and Ella, for some odd reason, she craves carrot sticks. She'll go through bags of them. I guess it's better than other stuff but... yeah. They crunch worse than anything else... they are so loud." Denny took in a deep breath and his shoulders relaxed again.

"The one thing though, is even through all of that, you have to learn to trust her."

"Well, yeah, I'd assume that much."

"You don't trust people very well." I said. I just knew that the way he acted around people. I don't know why he had opened up to me, but I knew that I was an exception. I understood completely. I wasn't much of a person to trust others either.

His eyes opened wide like he was going to defend himself, but they calmed again and he said, "That's true. I mean, it is something you need to learn and I never really learned it. It wasn't exactly part of the curriculum. You trust someone, it goes badly. Tried that a few times, and I'm pretty sure that there are still welts left on my back, although I hope to God that they're gone."

"It's been a couple years since you left school."

"Yes, but the only years that matter really to learn to trust people are those years. You trust your parents, next thing you know they send you away and never want to talk to you again. When you do try to talk to them they talk down to you, say you complain too much, that you'll be one of 'life's failures' if you don't turn out right. You try to make friends, but when you're not witty or handsome, it doesn't really work out… and you sure as hell can't trust adults." He shook his head and let out a sigh of relief that he had said that much.

"A bit of anger I'm sensing?"

"Some people call it upper middle-class angst." Denny said, laughing heatedly. "My father called it me being ungrateful and pathetic. He worked his ass off to send us to that school. My sister never complained, she let me do that. As soon as she hit fifteen, they were disappointed in her too, but up until that point I was the only one who fit into the category of 'life's failures.' Even more so now that I'm at this school."

"Why?"

He looked into the empty hallway briefly. There was a fluorescent light flickering uneasily. "I was raised to be a perfect gentleman, quiet, purposeful, a problem solver… but that also means cold, and here I am in bloody America, where people teach their kids to be kids and to express themselves as human beings. It's like a contagion here. It's so weird. People are oddly unconstrained around each other, around their superiors and my parents don't want that. My sister was enough of an unconstrained influence, but here I'm surrounded by it and it's really weird. It was culture shock at first, I didn't know what to do with myself. I still don't." There was a sheepish, nervous smile that came on his face and he avoided eye contact. "I can fit in, both at school, and here, with acting, that's why I do it. It's an excuse, and a controlled one, to be around people, to be involved with them and to interact with them. Otherwise I'm not very good at it."

"I could tell." I said. "There is a culture difference. My wife, when we had Benjamin, she had very strict rules. She didn't want him to grow up the way she grew up, but she didn't want him to be raised like an American either. There is ups and downs to both sides. A lot of times kids here are doted on and thus become ungrateful little bastards, they expect too much of other people and it's frustrating." I crossed my arms now too, which caused him to uncross his.

"That can't go for all kids though." Denny said. He looked out the window, he couldn't seem to keep his eyes on one place, or look at me for that matter. "But... I think I trust Ella. I know she trusts me. She has this collection of colored glass animals..." So did Tess. "She keeps them all over her apartment. She won't let anyone touch them. I was helping her clean one day and she let me dust them. They're her favorite things in the world, I don't know why, she just said that they used to be her grandmother's. I picked them up and she saw me holding a few and she didn't say anything. I know it's small... but... yeah..." He wrung his hands together as a wide smile broke across his face. I was always interested by how animated his face was when he spoke. His eyebrows would raise, his face would twist, he'd make facial expressions almost constantly... or there were other times when it was just his lips that were moving and nothing else; I didn't know the difference of place or time that caused that. He had a habit a swallowing like he always had a lump in his throat, down cast eyes (despite the fact that I kept telling him he needed to look up so people would respect him) and moving his chin side to side which was entirely too distracting, but I knew he had no clue he was doing it.

His eyes lit up for a moment and he looked at me before returning his eyes to somewhere at his hands. "I don't know how she's so patient, she's fully aware of how... well, I don't even know what the word is to be completely honest." He laughed. "I don't like people touching me, never have. I suppose I've never been used to it. So she makes an effort to like run up randomly behind me and jump on my back. First few times I thought I was going to have a heart attack and like fall over, not from her being on my back but because it happened. Then she'd like hold my hand, which makes me all nervous and clammy, which I know she finds horribly gross but she puts up with it. She also makes sure that I'm not sitting as far away as possible from her on the couch. I have a habit of that. It's not because I don't like her, but because that's the normal thing to do. She'll literally grab my arm and drag me over if she has to. Once next to her, I'm fine, it's just that I don't make the effort or initiation myself." He took in a deep breath. "But sometimes it's like we're already married. We bicker and stuff, but it's usually in good humor and we get over it quickly enough. Most of her problems are about me being so aloof, which I am completely aware of and am making an attempt to solve, but… it's just weird." He shook his head and said, "And since she's such a stickler about certain things… like me as a person, like hygiene and wardrobe and stuff, and I probably couldn't care less, she's finding ways to fix that."

I shook my head and smiled and said, "Good for her. Someone needs to do that."

"I don't see what the problem is."

"That haircut." I replied.

"I still don't understand… I got rid of the haircut, it's short! Ah, people are so odd. It's my head I should do what I want."

"Yes, but we still have to look at it, probably more than you do."

He touched the top of his head and sighed. "I feel like wearing that hat again just because you're mentioning it."

"Does Ella approve this haircut?" I asked.

"What's there to approve? My hair's just there like any other guy. Although she was getting quite annoyed with it being long for *Hamlet*. She kept saying that it shouldn't be so messy, but if I brushed it a lot it would look like creepily shiny, like when Aragorn in the *Return of the King*, when he's coroneted and his hair looks like that, well, mine looked like that and I just couldn't do it. It was a constant battle of what my hair should look like…"

"Then you know not to do that again." I said.

"Problem, I've been looking in other Shakespeare theaters to get a job. If that happens, then it will be a battle to deal with for quite a while." He shook his head. "And she likes to make fun of the stage makeup. I remember like two years ago when we started dating, she wanted me to meet her parents for dinner, but they had planned it for immediately after a show. I was so tired that…" He laughed nervously, "I still had old age make up on my face. Her parents were laughing so hard, they told me I should keep my face like that, it was so convincing I probably could have gotten a drink from the bar looking like that without getting carded." He was scratching his shoulder again.

"You have got to stop that." I said, eyeing his hand.

"What?"

"That!" I pointed at his hand.

"What am I doing?"

"Do you like have a perpetual rash on your shoulder or something?" I asked.

He looked confused. "No."

"Well, you're always scratching the same place on your back."

"Oh, well, I didn't know." He laughed nervously. I wondered why he was acting so weird today.

"What's going on?" I asked. My voice sounded completely fake. I hadn't really asked anyone with true concern in a while. It wasn't even true concern; it was more like curiosity.

His eyes lit up a little bit and he looked around nervously. "What do you mean?"

"You're acting odder than normal. Something's up. What is it?" I leaned back in my chair as if that was a sign of benevolence. "Is it your sister?"

"Well, yes, and no. It's kind of everything at the moment." After hearing about how oddly he was acting he proceeded not to show anything at all.

"You'll have to explain that to me a little bit." I replied.

He looked over to me and then back to his hands. "Bridget has surgery coming up. She's a bit nervous because they'll be trying to take out some tumors. The last surgery caused her so much pain that she would almost rather just let it be, but she's not going to get better without surgery. I know Ella's trying to help, she's been asking me to come over to her house more often. She's trying to get my mind off all the problems, but I feel more stressed out being away from my sister because I can't help her if I'm not there. Plus, there's school, and I'm trying to get through these classes so I can graduate, but I have to keep up my grades so that the grad school will accept me and keep the scholarship that they have proposed. There's just… too much, right now." He spoke so quickly I could hardly keep up. He looked back into the hallway.

"I think you should listen to Ella." I said. "And your sister."

He shook his head and said, "It's not that simple."

"Actually, it is. See, you need to trust that your sister knows what is best for her and you need to trust Ella that she's just trying to help and you need to not try to push her away. That is stressful for her as well. She probably has a lot on her plate as well." Suddenly I've become a damn therapist I thought. But this boy was stressed and on the cracks of freaking out and needed to talk. Although it seemed that he just needed cry or something, but I knew that he hadn't been taught how to do that either. Well, I'm preaching to the choir anyways.

"She does, she's a principle for this show at the ballet. It's a lot of work, a lot of leadership on her part. She's practicing late so many nights, sometimes I have to pry her away to get some rest. She's a perfectionist and all, especially with herself. She doesn't want to let anyone down in the production. It's not like what I do, I'm saying lines that are already written. I have a bit more control of my voice than she can expect from her body. She can't use her voice to tell the story." He looked back into the hallway. I was wondering what he saw, or what he thought he would see. "I don't know how Ella and Bridget can dance. Maybe I'm just too clumsy, but they just can speak through the music and through dancing."

"You have to speak through your body language as well, when you act." I replied.

"Yes, yes, but in a more human way. What they do, it's... the most human thing and so far from it that I don't know how to explain it. It's just beautiful. I could watch Ella dance all day if she'd let me, but she won't hardly let me come to rehearsals, says that it makes her nervous and she doesn't want any nerves." He smiled and said, "She has this friend of hers, her dance partner. I can't pronounce his name, he's Austrian. He's one of the nicest people I've ever met. He helps her be not nearly as nervous." He coughed a bit, and turned his head away, at such an angle that I didn't know if it was possible. "She helps me to be less nervous around people as well. It's this odd thing, that I can almost expect people to be looking at her and not me. She looks so much better than me."

"You can't possibly look that bad if you chose acting for your career choice. That's everyone staring at you. If you were butt-ugly you wouldn't have gotten any leads."

"Well, yes, but I can pretend it's not me that they are looking at. Besides, it doesn't matter what I look like then, I'm covered in a costume with makeup on. And like I said earlier, it's a safe environment, and controlled, to literally go barmy."

"And that you did." I said, smiling. "Have you seen the Mel Gibson version of *Hamlet*? I watched it the other day. I was curious to see what they did to it in movie form. Very good, but your performance was quite similar. You seemed to have taken an approach as he did to the character."

"I haven't seen it, although I probably should." He paused for a moment. "A lot of people play Hamlet as sort of a solemn man. I don't think he is, I think he's crazy to be quite honest and that was why one moment he was stark raving mad, and then another moment he was quiet and pondering... and he's mad but at the same time, as an audience, you see him as the sanest one there." He laughed and said, "I really had to get into his head, study the words to find clues about him... it was odd. It was like stepping into his shoes was an assault on my own character. I started to believe what he believed because he said it with such grace and purpose... and honestly, it was easy to believe that life was literally like a mortal coil and such. But at the same time, I'm very fond of life." He rubbed his shoulder, then stopped as soon as he realized that he was doing it.

"I suppose it's difficult to understand sometimes when you're only twenty-something."

"I suppose it is, but at the same time, I'm going to face death just as someone who is closer to it is. It's not like I'm escaping it by any means." He rubbed his hand together and touched his backpack's zipper a bit. "That and then there's my sister."

"Did she go watch the play?" I asked.

"Of course, of course. She liked it. She said Ophelia was her favorite character; said she wished there was more of her. She doesn't like watching me act like that on stage, it concerns her. It probably should but it was kind of nice. I don't get to freak out like that much." He kept speaking so quickly it made my head spin.

"You could, just not in front of your sister." I said.

"I'm not exactly in many other places when I'm not at school. If I just go somewhere and start screaming, people would be a bit confused, concerned, might call the police." I took a sip of my coffee which was going cold. I hated cold coffee. I stood up and put it in the microwave briefly before sitting back down to drink it. Now it was far too hot. There was never any happy middle. "When Bridget went to see the play, she knew what was going to happen, I told her enough about it, but she really was still concerned. Which is good, honestly, that means that I did a good performance."

"Yes, yes, I can say I was concerned for a moment as well. But then you got drunk."

"I think you'll hold that against me forever." Denny said.

"No, no, I understand you probably needed to blow off some steam."

"I feel so bad about it though, Mindy had to drag me into my house. I don't know, between leaving your house and getting to my door... I don't know, I just lost it. I probably passed out or something. I don't... I don't remember. She just left me inside my door. When I woke up Bridget was in front of me with her arms crossed. She wasn't happy." He laughed sadly and shook his head, rubbing his eyes. "I had this habit during school, before college, of drinking. It wasn't like a constant thing, but when I did, usually I'd get drunk enough to pass out. She was holding the... completely empty bottle of expensive wine in her hand and asked me where I got this, why it was empty, and... yeah..." He shook his head. "I don't remember if I did this, but she told me to apologize for drinking all your expensive wine. Then she told me, like a mother, how angry she was at my behavior for being so rash and all." He shrugged, still sadly smiling. "It'd been probably two years since that happened previously, so, she didn't have a lot to complain about, it's not like it was a regular occurrence."

"I think she has a point." I said. "You should listen to her. You need to learn to do things in moderation." I smiled and he bowed his head, holding in a chuckle. "You don't have to drink until you're dead ass drunk, and carpet grazing."

"I was on tile."

"Denny, you know what I mean. No tile grazing either."

"Even without parents I still have to hear all about it."

"You better the hell be listening too." I said. "Your sister knows what she's talking about."

"Only because she's done it a thousand times too. At least I didn't wake up somewhere with some stranger next to me."

"Don't judge." I said. "You can judge when you get old all you want. But right now, that's not your job. You might still do the same stupid thing some day too."

Denny sighed and shook his head and took a sip of water from an old plastic water bottle that had been used far too many times. It probably wasn't very healthy. "Fine, fine, fine, but it's not like she's much wiser than me. She only has a year above me. Hardly a year, eleven months at best."

"And far, far more experience, in what seems to be many things."

"Not that those things are always good..." Denny grumbled.

"That doesn't mean that she didn't learn anything. Just listen to her dammit." I said, frustrated, slightly annoyed.

"I'm her little brother, of course it's going to be difficult. I'm there to annoy the bloody hell out of her, I better be doing a fine good job of it." He smiled. "Keeps her spirits up."

"Now work on keeping your spirits up as well, while using spirits in moderation."

"Yes, yes, I can't afford wine anyways."

"Says the boarding school brat."

"Just because my parents have money, doesn't mean that I do." he said smartly. "Trust me, we're broke. Well, there is an occasional check in the mail, but it has instructions attached."

"Was there one that came in for new clothes yet?" I asked.

His eyes widened in disbelief. "You and everyone keeps saying that there is something wrong with my clothes."

"Then isn't it about time you listened to that? Are you deaf or something?"

"No, but my clothes are holding up just fine."

"You don't have to wear them till there are holes all over them. If you can see through it, it needs to be thrown away. Those shoes have been worn through the soles, that jacket... there are holes in that. You've had the pockets sewn back on a few times... and that one coat, there are fifteen different colors of thread holding the buttons on. Get new clothes."

"You pay too much attention." Denny said. "I don't have money for that yet. And I think that my clothes are just fine."

"You'll drive poor Ella up a wall."

"I wear my best clothes around her, so she doesn't get on my case."

"Good."

Chapter Sixteen

Denny came the next morning to take me to school. I planned on having a party in class today, with the goodies that were baked the previous day. It was going to be my last day at school. The dean and I spoke over the phone. It was clear my health was going downhill rapidly, and I wasn't performing my job to the best of my ability. I needed a reprieve and my students deserved better than what I could give them.

We went to the store and bought a few liters of soda and juice, cups, napkins, and forks before going. I went to my office to sit down for a moment. Walking through the store exhausted me sufficiently enough I needed to breathe. A few minutes later, Dr. Rogers knocked on the door. "Hello?"

"I have something for you. It's our parting gift."

I knew what it was. I'd seen this same trick on numerous professors before me. He handed me the watch box. I nodded, made eye contact, and silently he walked away. I opened the box, just to see what it would look like. Nothing special past a high-quality leather band. It was a sick, sick thing to be giving a dying man. A watch, as if it they thought I needed something to count how much time I had; to see how quickly or slowly the minutes were ticking by. I took it out of the box and put it in my pocket. I threw the box away.

Denny helped me set up the room before the class came. "We have like fifteen minutes before class starts. That didn't take as much time as I thought it would." I said, sitting comfortably in the chair we brought in. I couldn't stand longer than fifteen minutes. I really needed this chair.

"Uh huh, but I don't want people to know I made that stuff. You should tell them you made it all." he said with a smile.

"There is nothing wrong with being able to bake."

"I didn't say there was." he said, less than convincingly.

"You are one odd fellow." I said and sighed before looking up at the screen. "I decided to play music after I talk, from like the fifties to like the eighties."

"Any good music?" he asked.

"I'm not sure what that means." I said slyly. Some kids came in, looking confused and excited at the same time about there being food available.

Everyone was in on time. I was always happy when that happened. It was a rarity. I put my hands together and took in a deep breath. "So, for today I decided that all of you are working so hard that we should have a party." I could see everyone's face light up and they eyed the food. "Don't worry, I didn't make the food myself, you'll live." Denny shook his head and looked to his hands. "As you all know, though, I'm very ill. I've been getting progressively worse throughout this semester at a... rather alarming rate. This is the last class I will be teaching. Dr. Rogers will be taking over for the rest of the semester. I know that you have been working very hard on your papers, so I will still answer any emails that come my way. Don't hesitate to contact me at all. Hopefully I will be able to read some of your papers and be of assistance. He has been informed of everything you've been doing so far, though. It's just that I can't keep up with the work like I'm supposed to. I've been at this school for over forty years, I've picked up a few things that I would like to share with you."

Denny's eyes were wide and confused. He mouthed, 'you're quitting?' "While I have a captive audience, I might as well make the most of it. You all are extremely lucky to be in college. I understand that at times it feels required, and that it's the hardest job of your life, but right now you're young and you're in the prime of your life and you have the rest of your life ahead of you. This is still a privilege, being here, being educated. A lot of people don't have that opportunity. Please, embrace the opportunities like this. Don't spend all of it watching Netflix online, or dragging your asses over a bad breakup. There are more important things to life, I swear. You're here to get an education, and that's very important, but enjoy what you have. Those little things that you always get so hung up on, are really quite small and you actually don't have to spend all your energy worrying about them. I know that it's hard to believe, but I was your age once. It was a long time ago, and in what seems like a completely foreign land. I didn't have the opportunity to enjoy things like you did, I had to fight in a war, and then I had to get over having to have fought in that war. Most of you won't have to do that. I'm sure some of you have though. Most of you won't have to fight for anything for a while, just getting your education done and finding yourselves." I paused. "I haven't been able to get through much alone, myself, I've needed people to help guide me through things. It's important you recognize that. Please thank the people in your lives, appreciate them, and love them. I know it sounds cliché, but commit yourselves, it's worth it, I swear. I wish someone told me these things when I was younger. I was with my wife for almost fifty years. It was the best fifty years of my life. She taught me so much about women, which I thought I would never understand, and about humanity. She was always happy because she dedicated her time to others. I know that not all people are built that way, but if you are, please go out and use that gift you've been given. People need it. There are lonely people out there who are lost, confused, aching and all they need is for someone to just act like they care. But just as this is my last class, everyone, I just wanted to let you know what an old man thinks. There is no way for you to go back in time and fix things. I know that, and you know that, but the more time there is to go back in, the more it weighs on you and the worse you feel. I understand that completely and I know I'm preaching to the choir, because I still let those things get to me, but that's because it's been habit since I was your age. Don't let yourself do that. I understand that we all make mistakes and that's how we become who we are, but people are always changing, always evolving because of the circumstances surrounding them. Just know that you are one of those people, and your life goes by much quicker than you will ever know. I don't know where the past years have gone sometimes. What you are given isn't an extraordinary amount of time, but it is time and it has been given to you. It's a gift. You can't expect to be handed things. You can't expect to live a long life just by wishing for it. In every situation, you have to work your tail off to get what you really want. A mediocre effort leads to mediocre results, which is the bloody honest truth. I don't want you to be afraid of anything. The past is behind you, don't worry about that, you can't fix it, you can't alter it. It is as it is. The future is only effected by the present, so you need to pour your whole self into it. Go and be young, go and have fun, see places while you can. Do everything that you can, within reason of course, I'm sure as hell not advising you to jump off buildings, although if you are attached to a bungee cord and someone around you knows what the hell they're doing than I suppose it's ok. You get what I am saying. You all have great beginnings, and can go to amazing places. I must say, though, that there is always a way to get where you need to go." I looked at Denny, there was a sad smile on his face. He needed to perk up. "I could go on forever, but the purpose of today is for you to eat all this food that I brought and just take a break. You need it." I pointed at the table. "But one more thing," I said. I put the watch I received on the table. "This is what they give to professors who retire, cruel isn't it?" They laughed. "I'd love to see it broken, although I can't really do it myself."

One of my students, Michael, I had him in six classes

in the past four years. We knew each other well. His work ethic was extraordinary, as was his ability to research and delve into difficult subjects. He was one of those students worth the effort. He was going somewhere with life. He stood up and he walked down the middle of the classroom. He looked me in the eye once, flipped the watch upside down and took his fist to it. The watch was smashed to pieces. He wiped the bits and pieces off his skin. Other students came and destroyed it as well. It was a pile of metal and glass by the time they were finished. "Alright let's eat!"

The kids smiled and got up to retrieve food and the music played. Denny didn't get up, I motioned to him. "Come on, eat!" I said.

He looked startled by the words but nodded and got some of the cookies and sat down to eat them. Most of the people were mingling, laughing, eating and drinking the soda. He looked like he needed wine. He was alone. He was always alone. There were some students with questions about their papers. I was very happy to help. There was, though, this lump in my throat. I realized that I wasn't going to be able to do this again. I had to give up. I knew those were harsh words for the reality I was experiencing, but it was how I felt. I could see the door to my office. The whole thing was emptied of books. My banner was taken back to my house. The books were donated. The gargoyle was next to my wife. I was ready. I wasn't sure how much longer I had. My mind, though, was so intact, it didn't feel like it was going anywhere. That was the worst part about it. I felt like my mind could live on forever if it wasn't for my body and my grief.

Once the students left class, Denny expressed his anger toward me. "How could you just quit?"

"It's not exactly quitting." I said. "I literally am physically unable to do this job, Denny. I need to… slow down." He didn't look like he understood. "Denny, you know this as well as I do, I'm dying. I don't have the option of getting better like your sister does. I'm not going to get better, I'm going to get worse. I'm just trying to put things in order."

"You could have given me more warning than that." he said, with his eyes looking down to his hands that were folded on the table.

"What more warning did you need? I can't really walk; I can't hold anything… my voice sounds like a ninety-year-old chain smoker…" I took in a deep breath. "Besides I thought it was well timed." The watch. I made a joke. He didn't notice.

He shook his head and the smallest of smiles crossed his face. "Dr. Neal…" He looked up at me and asked, "Do you want to go somewhere?"

"What does that mean?" I asked, still sitting comfortably in the chair.

"Before it gets real bad." He stood up from his chair and grabbed his sweatshirt and put it on. "Well?" I thought it was pretty bad already…

"I… uh… I'm not sure I'm able." I replied.

"Where is your favorite place in the world?" he asked.

"The world?" I replied. "The coast, any coast. Just to see the water again. I'm tired of being landlocked."

"Then it looks like that's where we're going."

"And how do we manage to do that?" I asked.

"A car." he said simply.

I gathered up the broken watch and shuffled over to my office. I put the remnants on desk. It was the last thing left in my office. The door was open and Denny helped me outside. I wasn't going to be in the building ever again. I wasn't going to hear the odd ticking the front door made, smell the stale coffee from the faculty lounge... I wasn't going to have to try to squeeze into the tiny little stalls in the bathroom with the horrible, ancient, old yellow tile that had been there since I started working. I wouldn't be seeing the lovely secretary that worked in the office on the first floor who brought cookies at least once a month, and made sure that the mail got to my room so I didn't have to walk too far anymore. Such kind and interesting people I worked with, but that damn watch... I was done. I was angry with that, but I was glad that it was sitting on that desk, the same desk I had used to make my living on.

Denny asked, "What did you do that for? Leave the watch? Break the watch actually..."

He shoved his hands in the pockets of his jacket and looked down. I was walking slightly behind him if one would call my shuffling walking. "I... it just needed to happen Denny."

Chapter Seventeen

Denny was ruthless, but I wasn't capable of any trip. He didn't seem to care, he just kept saying, "We're going to get you to the coast." He wanted to put me in a chair. That seemed like the final mark on the fact that I was useless now. I couldn't even walk more than a few steps at a time. I didn't like being in the chair, but Denny kept saying it would make things easier for me. Well I didn't see how shrinking a few feet in size and not being able to reach anything was much of a help.

I held the book I just finished reading, *The Old Man and the Sea.* I read this book probably twenty times in my life. Each time I read it I understood the main character Santiago more and more. This was an old man facing his own death. I only wished I could have his strength, not only that of his body but of his mind too. He was strong enough to accept death, but also to protect his life at all costs, to hold onto it and keep on fighting. I wasn't like that. I wanted to be though. He seemed like he had the toughness of a man who lived his entire life fighting the ocean and nature. I spent my entire life fighting books.

Denny brought my bag to the passenger seat. Racer jumped in the back as soon as he opened the door and stared happily out the window. Apparently, he was coming with. Denny smiled, petting the dog. "Are you coming, Dr. Neal?" he asked walking to the door.

"I'm coming, I'm coming. It's not like I have much of a choice, you're making me go in this godforsaken chair." I sighed, wheeling myself forward. I told Denny I could do it myself, it would give my arms something to do, but they weren't very strong either and I was extremely tired.

"I got it." Denny said, about to let go of the door.

"No, no, I can do it." I snapped. "Go hold the door open." I looked behind me to make sure all the lights were off, and everything was in order when I went over the bump and onto the sidewalk. He then started pushing the wheelchair. "Denny, I said I can do it." I repeated. Het let go and went to open the door to the back of the car so we could put the chair in there. I stood up and out of the chair and into the car while Denny situated everything.

"Looks like we are ready to get on the road," he said, backing out of my driveway. I sighed and took in a deep breath. Racer licked my ear and I laughed a bit. Denny rolled the window down enough so Racer could stick his head out. Once he did, he was quite happy with himself.

"Racer is one goofy boy." Denny stated.

"Yes, yes, he is." I missed Titan, but I knew that wherever he was, he was probably with Tess and Tess was probably with Benjamin, at least I hoped that was the situation. "You should tell me more about this Ella girl."

He laughed a bit and looked to the left and turned. "I told you plenty." Silence. "Fine, well, uh... hmm..." He thought for a little while. "I met her because of my sister.

When Bridget first got diagnosed I was uh… a bit overprotective. I drove her everywhere because I didn't want her going places by herself in case something happened. I drove her to school and to her dance practice and Ella was usually there, and at the time they were good friends. Ella asked me what was going on and why Bridget was missing so much. I told her, partially at least, and we talked, and we talked some more. I started coming earlier and earlier to pick Bridget up so I could watch Ella dance." He smiled sheepishly. "I think she noticed because she asked me if I'd like to go to dinner, and I kind of had issues saying yes because Bridget is right, I'm not good with talking to girls that I like. The way she was smiling though implied she liked me which made it worse. And I was laughing too much and probably turning colors, but God, Dr. Neal, Ella is gorgeous." He looked over at me and I nodded in agreement so he would keep talking. "I didn't want to know what Bridget would say about me dating Ella, well anyone actually. You see how she is." I nodded again.

He took in a deep breath and fell silent for a moment while we turned onto the highway. "I don't know how she could possibly know me as well as she does. She always knows exactly what I'm thinking."

"Well you do have a very expressive face." I said. "It doesn't take a lot of guessing."

"I do? Well, I suppose I should…"

"I didn't say it was a bad thing."

"Although I think the only nice thing I really did for her was the morning after I stayed over for the first time I got up early and made her some chocolate chip pancakes with some hot coco. I'm not sure that she drank any of the coco, but I made it. Ugh… now that I think about it… I must have looked like hell, I was walking around, and my hair was all unbrushed,"

"You comb your hair? Your hair looks questionable enough."

"Let me finish, let me finish. I had my hideous glasses on because I couldn't see through my contacts after sleeping with them on, and then I was walking around in my underwear because I didn't want to wake Ella up by going back in the room to change and rummage through all my crap. I did the dishes from dinner the night before, we had lasagna, it was really dried on… but I was listening to show tunes and singing along, I didn't know I was that loud but it woke her up… so maybe it wasn't all that nice because I woke her up…" He laughed and shook his head. Three things in one motion. Huh.

"That can't possibly be the only thing you've done that's nice."

"Well I don't know if this counts as nice…" He took in a breath and turned a corner on the street. "But it sure was funny. Around Christmastime I took her to an ice skating rink, you know the one in the center of town? You know how beautiful it is when it's night outside and all the lights are so bright and colorful and sparkling? I wanted to show her because she's never gone before. It was perfect, except that she'd never actually gone ice skating before. She was going to give it a try, but the fact that the most graceful person I know, a classically trained dancer, and a principle at a ballet, was completely out of her element. I thought it was hilarious how she was falling over and really having a tough time of it. She looked like a giraffe on ice. I know it's horrible of me, but she was holding onto me so she wouldn't keep sliding all over, and that was really nice. She ended up getting the hang of it, thankfully, but it was such a good time. We went a few weeks after that she seemed to have no problems, in fact she was quicker than me. I think she probably practiced in between those two times..."

"Oh Denny..." I laughed and shook my head, my voice cracked a bit and turned into a wheeze. After clearing my throat, it sounded like it was able to make words again. "So, you think she practiced?"

"Well, I wouldn't put it past her. She's competitive, which is a good thing for her career, but she really doesn't like being bad at anything. Even when we go to the arcade, or bowling, or anything else, she has to win. If she doesn't win she gets angry. It's funny when she gets angry because she's adorable and starts having conniptions but at the same time I don't like her being angry about anything. I usually either make sure she wins, or I let her. A lot of times, though, she's good enough to beat me... especially when we go bowling."

"You don't like bowling?" I asked.

"I'm absolutely wretched at bowling. It keeps going in the gutter thing, always goes left, unless I try for it not to go left and then it goes really, really right. Although I think it would be really fun to take her snowboarding some time. I don't suck at that. She hasn't tried that yet. Or skiing, either of which are great fun and she'd be falling all over the place again which is always entertaining." He shook his head, speaking quickly, almost erratically. "She really is great to be around. One of the first times I really spoke to her was right after Bridget got diagnosed, like I mentioned. Bridget called our parents and told them, and she was honest that she had HPV first and they started… ripping her apart over the phone. She just held it away from her ear. It was close to Christmas. We didn't go home until Easter that year. Ella asked if we wanted to come to her house for Christmas and we did. She even let us stay over… which is odd because she has three brothers and they live in this tiny little house with no room to fit all the people in her family to begin with, but her parents were so welcoming. Bridget wasn't handling anything well around that time. She was still dancing despite the pain and despite what the doctors were telling her and people were noticing. Ella didn't want to anger Bridget so she asked me… I remember that we were sitting in the garage while her father was out with her brothers, they went to the bar or something like that. I remember because she was wearing this horribly ugly Christmas sweater that she'd worn since she was twelve every Christmas, it was red with a white cat on it. It was really distracting. She told me that she noticed Bridget was having some difficulties. And I told her about the diagnosis. I told her Bridget wasn't supposed to be dancing anymore. But that was Bridget's life…"

He took in a deep breath and slowed down on the street, his foot had been a little heavy on the gas pedal. "Bridget didn't know what else to do with her time. She doesn't really like books or movies; she likes to keep moving. She wasn't supposed to run that much, although they told her to walk. She'd end up walking miles in one day and be exhausted and in horrible pain by the end of the day to the point that she couldn't walk the next, and she'd get these whole body cramps and be screaming… the only thing that would help were hot baths, that and some wine, but it wasn't exactly in the budget. Neither were, so much water is expensive. But Ella gave Bridget some wine for Christmas that year, and she hugged me." He smiled and said, "She told me that if I needed any help to just call her. I would've, I really would've earlier, but Bridget wanted to hide all of her symptoms from the people she worked with. She didn't want to be seen as weak, even though she felt weak. Ella understood though, and she just wanted Bridget to have a friend by her side… Bridget, though, she kind of cut everyone off by the time she had to stop dancing. I suppose it was easier for her that way. She was going to be fired anyways because she couldn't keep up with everyone else, and she couldn't hide the cramps and pain much anyways. She has an expressive face too." He took in a deep breath. "I think it was the second to last time Bridget was at practice that Ella asked if I wanted to go on a date."

He laughed a bit in memory. "It was the weirdest first date I've ever been on, according to my sister I haven't been on many… but Ella, I guess we knew each other enough that it wasn't like we were introducing ourselves. She was asking so many questions about my sister and I asked her if she just wanted to date my sister or something. I think her response was something like 'well, I can't ask her any of these questions so I'm asking you.' I was so confused, but it turned out alright. I embarrassed myself to pieces because for some reason I decided to eat spaghetti. There needs to be some kind of manual that says that you don't eat spaghetti on a first date, or second. Or ribs... we had ribs a few weeks later. I mean really, it was embarrassing. It made her laugh though, which was nice and lightened the mood."

"You are one interesting little man." I sighed. "You really are."

"She is one interesting woman."

"I can imagine."

"It was like two weeks ago we were sitting on the couch watching a movie. I don't even remember what movie, but she yanked on my arm and demanded I sit closer to her. I was perfectly comfortable on the other side of the couch, but I didn't get much of a choice. I guess she wanted to cuddle or something, I don't really get the point of that... but she was trying to get comfortable and she rearranged me and put her head on my stomach and she had a conniption, just like she does when she loses. She yelled, 'you're supposed to be a pillow! What is this? Where's the pudge?' I was really confused... between the sword fighting, yelling for hours on end for Hamlet, and carrying my sister around the house, I guess I wasn't much of a pillow anymore. She walked to the kitchen and shoved popcorn in my face. It was really strange... so I just shoved a real pillow under my shirt and she laughed and used me as a pillow."

"Strange... so strange..."

"I really, really do think she's a better person than I am. She gives way more than I do. She like... it's weird, she absorbs the stress; other people's stress. She will just sit there and listen to me vent for hours and she doesn't get frustrated or angry with me... I mean that day she kept telling me to stop worrying and to focus on her for once... but there is always so many things on my mind that it's really difficult. She understands though. I'm way too lucky." He shook his head and looked out the car window for a moment.

"I think it's been like two years now that we've been together. Ella's such a strong woman and she is aware of what she wants for her life and her career and she knows how to get there. She's very driven but she's so full of life. I don't think that anything can bring her down, really. She just seems to have her own source of energy and I only wish that I could be like that."

"You are fine just the way you are." I said. "You try, that's all that matters."

"Thanks, Dr. Neal." he said, but his thanks didn't sound convincing in the least.

"And I'm glad you've been with this girl that long. I was concerned that she was just a fling or something."

"Oh no, no, no, we've been together for a while. I don't think I could do flings very well, honestly. I'm kind of a sucker for commitment, well that and I've never done a fling before, she's the first girl, and hopefully only girl, that I've been with... and I think she is looking for commitment too, which works, but it's a good thing she's the louder one of the two of us because two quiet people together would be really odd."

"You're not that quiet." I said. "You're only quiet when you want to be."

"I'm only loud when I want to be, actually." he corrected. His eyes were bright and sparkling from the sun. I wished that I could be that full of life. He wanted to have even more life in him, like Ella, but I just wanted what he had. I didn't have hardly any left. I was so tired, and frustrated because I was so tired. I couldn't sleep it off either because I just wouldn't wake up.

I stared out the window, watching little towns go by and the coast growing closer. I could see the bright blue and white in the distance, and the birds flying above. "So, what are you going to do now that you are retired?" he asked it like it was an exciting question.

I wanted to answer honestly and say: die, but that wouldn't do him any good. "I suppose I'm going to do this."

"And then?"

Die, I thought again. What else was I supposed to say? "Just relax." Yes, my entire body, down to every last muscle and nerve ending until they don't function at all anymore. "What are you going to do this summer?" I asked.

"I'm going to sell my soul to the theater and get a job there if I'm lucky. I know some people who work there and there are summer productions. I need something to do but I still need to help Bridget out. I don't know if she's going to get better or not. I need to plan for that." Amen, I was feeling the same way, except I wasn't really expecting to get through the summer. It just didn't feel like a reality. "She's hanging in there well enough though; she's getting enough food in her, although she got pretty dehydrated for a while. The doctors said that the masses aren't growing anymore. The cancer has metastasized though, and they don't know if they can destroy it in all the places. They have lots of plans, though."

"How much is she willing to go through?" I asked.

His voice went quieter and the light in his eyes dimmed. "I don't know. She's so young; she's too young. She needs to fight so she can live out the rest of her life."

"Is that the only reason, Denny?" I asked. He didn't respond. "I know you want her there for you as well, just know what she's going through, if it is worth it or not."

"It must be worth it." he said strongly. "She's too young, Dr. Neal. She's too young."

"That's not exactly how it works. Being young doesn't mean that you won't die."

"Don't say that please..." he mumbled, desperation entering his voice. "My sister doesn't deserve this."

"No one deserves to be sick like that, Denny. No one does." My voice was soft but I knew the weight behind what I was saying. "I wish there was a better explanation than that, or something that makes more sense, but it will never make sense. I've been asking the same question my entire life. It's just a fact that we aren't going to live forever. Some of us have more time than others and some of us go easier than others, but we all go." I paused. "And I'm going to go pretty damn soon."

"Dr. Neal..."

"You know it as much as I do. Anyone who is living is dying, it's just who is approaching it sooner than others. I think you have plenty of time left, Denny. Take it, go have fun, go make lots of money and become famous or something, I don't know. It's your choice, but if you waste it, I sure as hell will find a way to haunt your ass."

He laughed a bit and said, "Well, I wouldn't want that to happen."

"You'll have a bitter old man pestering you." I paused and thought about it and laughed a bit. "Wow, that would be horrible. My father told me before I went off to Vietnam that if he died before I came back, that he'd haunt me, just because he said it would be fun; said he'd be one of those ghosts that does stupid stuff like steal your keys just to make you remember that they are there, always watching you. God, I was terrified that would happen, so I told him that he had to be abnormally careful. He asked me what I would do if I got a bullet in me. I just said that if that happened, I already did my time in hell, and that I should just go straight the other direction. After I came back I told him that I'd rather just sleep off the rest of eternity. He said that was too boring, I had to choose something else. He said it would be funny if I haunted a church, just walk up to the people in there, decide to glow white or something and see how confused they get."

Denny looked concerned and replied, "I don't understand you." I looked out the window to the bright, beautiful sun and the blue, blue sky that I had missed so dearly. It was oddly warm out, and it was perfect.

"I don't think you need to…" I said. "You know, my son and I always talked about what we'd do if we were ghosts when he was younger. He said he thought they were scary. He didn't want to be scary, so he'd just do good things for people, try to move things out of their way if they almost trip, or help them find things…"

Denny slowed the car down and he took in a deep breath and looked over to me for a brief moment. "I don't want to think of you as a ghost."

199

"Is that because you don't want to think of me as dead? What else am I going to do? That's probably what all the people do when they don't have any other expectations."

Denny slowly nodded. "Then please, pick something else."

I pet my dog for a moment. He seemed to get even happier by touch. "Don't mind me." I said. We reached the coast, and it was a rather rocky beach, but it worked. There was no one here, even on such a beautiful day. Denny turned the car off and gathered my wheelchair. He let Racer out. The dog immediately started running toward the water like a maniac.

I shuffled into the chair and said, "I don't think I can push myself over these rocks, Denny."

"Alright." he said and he wheeled me next to the water. I could smell the salt in the slightly chilled air that whipped around me. I took in a deep breath and felt a click in my chest, a release.

"Can you put the chair in the water a little bit Denny?" I asked. He didn't say anything but pushed me forward. I could feel the water touch my toes. It was cold, but perfect. The entire place was vacant of all human life, although white birds swarmed ahead, far off in the sky, ducking in and out of the clouds. I could see little sea shells in the water, hidden amongst the small rounded pebbles that covered the ground. The water was very clear.

"I don't think I dressed well for the occasion..." Denny mumbled, rolling up his trousers. I reached down to touch the clear water. I wanted to stand up, and feel the small pebbles on my feet. I put both hands on the chair since Denny was busy and I stood up. I felt shaky and unsure on my feet, yet exhilarated. I smiled and walked forward a bit until I was up to my shins in the water. Racer stood next to the water, he had never seen such a thing before and didn't know what to do. He looked nervous and touched the water, backed up and then rushed in after me. I laughed and he came to me, splashing all over the place.

I stood in a suspension... there was a feeling that I was inbetween life and death. I sure as hell couldn't live very much anymore but I sure as hell wasn't dead yet. I was trapped in my body which was being eaten by age... I was disappearing and fully aware of it. As I stepped forward again, I wondered why it was that I couldn't be given some kind of dementia instead. Almost the same thing probably happened to the body, at least it caused death, but the person with it was spared from the awareness of what was happening to them. I've seen it many times in faculty at school, and family members. It's excruciating for the family... but I didn't have any family who could see it. I could just be clueless. But no, instead I had to be given a curse of suffering through the awareness of my own demise. It wasn't like I was going as quickly as some. I was just waiting.

Racer touched me and even that small touch made me fall down. I held myself up in the water. "Dr. Neal!" Denny called out.

"I'm fine!" I called to him and I leaned back in the water, letting it soak over me and I stared up at the sky. I let my head go under for a moment and opened my eyes and saw the sunlight fracture everywhere, moving in dots of white light. I took some breath and sat up. Here I was, touching the water and touching the earth. I'd become these things someday, go back to the ground just like millions of people before me. It had given me life and with its grace, would take it back. The water embraced me, so familiar and so living. I never thought I would feel so perfect or at ease. I felt like I could do anything. I stood up and began to run forward. I didn't think it was possible and in all honesty I knew I'd gone mad. I couldn't do this, but I was given something for just a moment and I was going to take it. I felt strong. I didn't feel young again, in fact I felt quite my age. I felt like I was a dead man. I felt like I wasn't in my body anymore, like I didn't have to be in it. Like I could just fly away. Like I could see my wife, and my son and that I could join them wherever they were, even if it was in the depths of the sea in front of me. I knew I'd done nothing to deserve what they had, I was not that good of a person but I so wanted to see them. To feel like I wasn't trapped inside myself anymore.

I stopped and stretched out my arms and looked up to the bright, beautiful sky and saw the birds going overhead of us and I took in a deep breath again, feeling my lungs fill with air. I knew I was alive. I knew that I was inside of my body as frail as it was, and I was going to kill it doing this, but I didn't care one slight bit anymore.

Chapter Eighteen

I could feel the frailty creep back into my bones. I hunched back over, my legs and my arms trembled, and I could feel the stiffness and pain reenter my body. My chest became hard and it was difficult to breathe. I fell over, but it wasn't out of joy this time. I lay in the water and stared, in pain, in awe of how mad I must have been. I couldn't even move. I just froze in the water, feeling it lap against my papery skin. I could taste the bitter saltiness in my mouth, as if it was clinging to me, forming a shell. I dug my hands into the pebbles and held onto them.

Everything disappeared for a few more moments. It was just me and this sky and this water and I was still away from my wife and my son. I was still away from what I loved and I was still trapped. I hated this body. I hated what it did to me. I hated what I did in it. I hurt people. I hurt myself. I was a bitter old man. I still was a bitter old man, bitter about my bitterness. God just kill me now, I begged. Why are you keeping me here like this? What is the purpose? Please... but if there was any purpose to anything, I was supposed to stay on this earth longer.

The world rushed back to me, not just my body. I could

hear Racer jumping in and out of the water, splashing Denny who had fallen otherwise quiet. I didn't want to move. I felt humiliated and ridiculous for the way I acted. I sat up a bit and turned my head to Denny who was throwing sticks for Racer and smiling and mostly wet from the dog. He was so happy, so calm, so ignorant and yet he truly wasn't. His eyes told me everything and even in this moment of joy he was fully aware. He knew what was going on in the world. He'd seen his sister suffer too much. I could see it in his eyes. He knew everything she felt. He was suffering right along with her and was ready to take on some more. There was this innocence though that was on him, it was an innocence from suffering and taking it without question, without hesitation or anger. He stood with the upmost confidence, but it was quiet, it was reasonable. He stood differently now than when I met him, he wasn't protecting himself as he once did. He didn't keep his arms close to his body, one always holding his shoulder. He stood as if nothing could hurt him in this instance, and yet everything was. The entirety of his future was bearing down on him and it wasn't going to stop anytime soon. He was too young for that. I supposed that was why he didn't think his sister could die. There were too many expectations for her to achieve just yet as there were for him.

I didn't want him to see me like this. He didn't need this. I sat there and composed myself, splashing water on my face to wake me up. I didn't have enough strength to get back in the chair, but I tried my darndest but was at its base when I was completely and utterly too exhausted to move. Denny didn't say anything he just put a hand under each arm and lifted me into the chair and went back to playing with the dog. The action took hardly any effort. I stared ahead, wondering how I could get into that deep, deep ocean, just to stay there, never to leave.

After a while I could feel Denny pulling the chair out of the water and onto the shore. "Are you ready to go?" he asked. I nodded. Denny put towels down all over his car so that none of us harmed the upholstery. I couldn't even focus, move, process information. It was like my brain left with the rest of my body.

Denny drove with the radio on. "I'm sorry." I managed to say.

"Don't be." he replied. "That needed to happen."

After arriving home, I returned to a stack of sticky notes and continued to write on them. The fridge, since it was relatively new, would go to the donation center so a family who needed it may have it. The same would go for all of my good dishes and silverware. The radio was ancient, so I wanted it to go to Dr. Rogers who studied the World War era, and this was from that time period. He might enjoy the equally old record player. I had more books inside my house and thus more for the library. The furniture would be sold and added to the total value that the estate would be worth. Everything was covered in sticky notes. Then there was one big set of sticky notes that was on the door leading to the outside, "The dog will go to Henry Helling." I didn't think he needed a dog, but I sure as hell wasn't letting Racer go to the pound. He was trained to help people who were sick.

The accountant came within a few days. It was almost April now. I looked up the school Denny was attending and the neighborhoods around it, how much rent cost, utilities, and so on. We calculated up how much that would cost over the three years he planned to be there, and then startup costs for his life afterwards. We figured out how much his sister's medical costs would be over a two-year period, and finally came up with a number. I asked him how much he thought the house was worth as well as the car and the bicycles in the garage and the furniture. The money that Denny would need would go to him and the rest would be donated to a fund that would be for scholarships at the college I worked at, specifically, though, for humanities majors with specific needs for help. I had a will drafted by my lawyer soon as I was going downhill quickly.

Chapter Nineteen

Denny did arrange for me to meet Ella. We were going to meet at the cafeteria. Denny dropped me off at HBC early and was going to go pick her up from her brother's house a few miles away. I admired the trees I knew I would miss. From the large picture window I sat against, I could see the large sprawling park. The park was cultivated by the founder: Daniel Martin Hunting. Amongst the vast array of trees were the original, massive, ancient white pines that towered in the air some scraggly now, and others compact and busy. Another pine that added color to the winter landscape that had thankfully left us were scots pine. These were far less Christmas tree like, standing tall up in the air with narrow, white trunks that only produced limbs halfway up. A small cluster of pine like European larch trees drooped sadly in the corner of the park, covering vast areas of land, but looking like they were being held down by a heavy wind.

Assisting in feeding the massive, fat, squirrel population were the sprawling, shade providing black walnut trees that many students used to hold up their portable hammocks. It was funny when some of them came in with goose eggs on their head from being bonked with a falling walnut. Also feeding the large population of squirrels and destroying bare footed walkers was the bitternut hickory tree. The oldest ones were tall and heavy, with bright green small leaves. Nearest to the campus were the paper birch trees, small trees that had white, peeling bark. They were great for climbing, having otherwise smooth bark, and nice curved branches. In the springtime there were usually a few students stationed amongst the lower branches. They gave the brightest fiery colors in the fall, brightening the campus intensely.

Stationed in the center of the park was a collection of oak trees. The largest was a white oak that's trunk was as wide as my car. It was old, gnarled, covered in bulbous sores, but otherwise healthy. The thick heavy branches drooped down and were sturdy for climbing. Attached to this singular tree were swings that people lounged and played upon. Included in the oak collection were red oaks, black oaks, and pin oaks, generally covering the ground in acorns. The black and pin oaks were thinner, higher, and the squirrels liked chasing each other more on these trees than everywhere else really.

The overall widest tree was a horse chestnut, sprawling across a space the size of the library's biggest lounge. It was very dome like and turned a startling golden color in the fall. It was beside a collection of beautiful lacebark pine that had redneck camo patterned bark. I supposed it was smooth and beautiful enough that a good hundred names of couples had been detailed on it- usually carved with car keys.

Along the flower garden path were some black willow trees, with small, pin like, drooping leaves that let a lot of bright sunlight through that during a golden sunset, would shimmer along the ground. Near to the library were some cottonwood trees, giant, scraggly, and lopsided. The seeds would land everywhere, covering the place in a downy, fluffy, white, sneeze inducing seed.

The beautiful park was filled with kids right now, playing with a Frisbee, lounging on blankets with books, sleeping in hammocks, and a few people playing the guitar. I used to spend afternoons there with the dogs, throwing a ball for them to catch, walking them, letting them sniff all the surfaces and chase some of the squirrels. It'd be nice to do again.

I sat in the same booth that I normally sat in with my food on my plate and my travel mug. I didn't know how to eat this without making a fool of myself in front of everyone. It was an adventure enough just trying to dish the food out to myself and carry the plate over here, get silverware and fill the mug up with something to drink. I didn't know how such simple things could become so difficult so quickly.

I saw the pair walk through the door. Denny looked like himself when he was around lots of people: deflated, passive, quiet. She, though, this Ella girl, walked with such confidence and grace that it was almost scary. She was muscular and perfectly in order. She was classically trained. How the hell did Denny end up with her? Damn.

They sat down in front of me. Denny had his usual greasy sandwich while she had chicken noodle soup, a few crackers and some carrots. I'd die if I had to eat like her. "Hi Dr. Neal, this is Ella. Ella this is Dr. Neal."

"It is nice to meet you." she said and we shook hands.

"And you as well. Your name is very interesting." I stated. Denny's face fell just by my tone of voice. I'd laugh if it wouldn't ruin the moment.

"It is?" she asked, her head leaning to one side. Her face was very soft, calm, but her voice had some command to it.

"Yes, it is a king's name, an Anglo- Saxon Northumbrian king's name. Many kings had the name of Ella, or variations of it such as Aella and Aelle." Denny's eyes bugged out for a moment, wondering where this was going. He then took in a deep breath and shook his head. He had read the books I had given him. Good for him. "The last Northumbrian king with that name, though, poor wretch, got an eagle carved onto his back with knives."

Her eyes then bugged out very similarly to Denny's as she was about to eat her food. She put the spoon back in the bowl. "I'm glad that I have such an interesting name."

"I have the name of some kings too!" Denny stated, trying to be interesting or changing the subject.

"And we all love Henry VIII because he's so much fun." I replied.

"I don't think people give him enough credit." Denny stated.

"Really?" Ella and I both said in unison, she turned her head to look at him with disapproving eyes.

"You of all people should give this man more credit

than he has been given..." Denny looked at me. "He did more than that, he started the reformation in England,"

"Yes, because he wanted to divorce his wife and Rome wouldn't let him." Ella said, shaking her head in response.

"Another history lover?" I asked, smiling.

"Some." she replied. "But I'm sorry, I don't like *Henry VIII*, his children, fine, they are reasonable, but not him."

"Elizabeth I, just reasonable? She was a very interesting human being." I pressed.

"Of course, a patron of the arts." Then she looked at Denny and repeated his own words, "You of all people should like that."

"Me of all people? You're a dancer, which seems like 'arts' to me." He looked hilariously defiant to her tone of voice, and crossed his arms for a brief moment, but then uncrossed them after staring at his sandwich for a little while.

"Let me rephrase myself, *Elizabeth I*, Shakespeare, you happen to have been very involved in Shakespeare... *Hamlet? Macbeth* last year, and *Richard III* at some point, right?" she stated.

"Yeah..." he sighed and shook his head with a smirk on his face. I still had yet to understand how he ended up with this girl. She continued to talk about how she'd been involved in dance since she was a little girl, and never lost interest, in fact, she loved performing so much that she was doing it as a career. Good luck, I thought, that probably won't get anyone very far, but good luck.

She had to leave very soon though since she was late for a practice. Denny smiled, watching her leave. "How did that happen?" I asked.

"How did what happen?"

"You ending up with her."

"Is it that much of a shock? Really people…"

My eyebrow raised, at least I was thinking that they did and I cocked my head to one side. "Why is it that I believe your sister more than I believe you when it comes to you and girls."

"I don't know." He sighed. "Well how good could you have possibly been with the ladies?"

"Quite wonderful." I replied. "I was married for fifty years."

"Before that." he sighed and took the last bite of his sandwich.

"Well I was only with Tess. I met her in college, like I told you. In fact our first real date she took me dancing. It was embarrassing because I grew up with parents who were against dancing and I never had the opportunity to learn. She assured me that all would be fine once we got to the club and she would teach me. It was a swing dance place, so it required rhythm. I still, to this day, do not know how to dance… but I supposed that I must have been charming enough." I took a sip from the mug, very careful not to spill. "Do you know how to dance?"

"Well, Ella has actually dragged me to lessons. She said that if we go somewhere that requires dancing she doesn't want to be embarrassed by me. It's mostly ballroom dancing and stuff like that. Otherwise my dancing abilities are few and far between. She thinks it's charming when I sing in the car."

"Ah really? Because you sound better than the people on the radio?"

"Potentially. She doesn't sing. I've probably never heard her actually singing to anything and every time I ask her she kind of like freaks out and says no one needs to hear her. She tells me she sounds like a dying walrus but I don't believe her."

I laughed a bit and put the cup down. "Oh really?"

"Can't exactly corroborate her story."

"Two years ago you sang O Holy Night for Vespers with someone, who was it?"

His eyes opened wide and he said, "You went to that?"

"My wife made me." I replied.

"I was singing with my sister." He laughed. "She loves that song."

"You made my wife cry every year you sang, but that year…" I mumbled. I looked out the window briefly at the buds on the trees and sighed.

"I made her cry? Like a good cry right? I hope I didn't sound so bad she cried, sorry."

"She was happy. I thought that she was like going to go into hallucinations about actually seeing angels and crap. I don't know what was going on in her head at the time. But you did well. I didn't know it was your sister you sang with."

"She doesn't look like that anymore…" Denny sighed. "She had long dark brown hair then, it was gorgeous, and she was probably thirty pounds heavier than she is now. I couldn't pick her up then. I could probably pick her up with one arm now."

"Well I think that is both her being smaller and you being stronger."

"True, true." He laughed and said, "Actually I was starting to work out then just because I wanted to…" He was still laughing. "I wanted to impress Ella, and you know the guys she works with are like massively built and I'm like…" He just put his arms out and looked at himself, "Well I look different now, but I was just kind of this skinny kid that my sister could have picked up and thrown me across the room really." He paused and was poking at his beans now with a fork. "But she was diagnosed with HPV two days before we sang that. She meant probably every word she sang. She had been contemplating things a lot just in those two days, because she knew she was sick before then. It was just that the doctors had to tell her how sick she really was." He looked up and said, "I suppose we were both in the same boat that night."

"Not exactly." I sighed. "I had to listen to my wife's sermon the rest of the night… she was in this kind of desperate frenzy to make sure she was going to heaven and to make sure that I would eventually too."

"Did you not listen to her?" he asked.

"Why would I listen to her?" I answered. "She was delusional at that point. Besides I had been hearing it my entire life…" I took in a deep breath and said, "The only thing that ever got me to listen after I was in Vietnam was while we were in a hospital at the end of her life. Tess was on about fifty thousand medications to help with the pain.

She was just a sack of pain at that point. She was in and out of consciousness and when she was conscious she was far from lucid." I took in a breath and moved my plate aside.

Denny sighed and said, "Eat some of it."

I shook my head and picked up the piece of bread and nibbled at it. "But one day there was this doctor coming in. He wasn't wearing a name tag or anything. He just walked into the room and he shook my hand and said that he knew I didn't like doctors but he was just there to help Tess feel better. Tess was lucid and awake and she looked... not so bad really. They talked for a little while and I was just blown away by the fact that she was alright. She was back for a little while. The man was really nice and I can remember his voice perfectly. Very smooth, very basic really, but at the same time overly comforting. After he left I went to the front desk and asked who the doctor was and they just said that they didn't know what I was talking about. Tess was awake for another day like that... then she just didn't wake up again, she was in a fully brain-dead coma till she died, so completely unaware of the pain her body was in. It was like someone had given her a gift."

Denny nodded and said, "And you still don't believe in miracles?"

"Do you?"

"I believe that something could save my sister." he replied very quietly, nervously.

"I think that is just your... youthful hope."

"No, it's my faith." he replied staunchly.

"And I don't have any, not in God, or in humanity, or in anything." I sighed and leaned back.

His brow furrowed in concern. "None at all? How does that even work?"

"I don't know, spend two years in Vietnam, and have your son go through exactly what you had to go through, but get blown to bits instead. Things change under that lens, Denny."

"But that doesn't give you any reason not to believe in anything at all." he sighed, slouching, resting his head in his hands.

"I believe in science. Science is proven, it proves that we are nothing but animals, which I've seen and can understand. It is just humanity's nature that makes us believe in more order and in something more than what actually exists."

"So... I..." he wasn't grasping the concept.

"I suppose that I believe in nature as a being, as something that was always here and that will be after us if that is something."

"No, it's not, because although I do believe in something... I suppose, supernatural, but I do know that there was something before the earth. What I do know is that if there is just nature, and nature is of itself as a being, that would require the system, which you are describing to be completely interlocked. Every event would be a necessary product of the system. Which would not give humans free will or account for the randomness that we know actually exists." He took in a breath and put his plate aside now. "But if something exists on its own, it must have always existed and without end because it cannot cease to be and it cannot begin again. So it must have always been there and we know that it has not."

"I'm not talking about nature like the trees in the birds, I'm talking about the laws of nature."

"The Big Bang, or whatever it is called now, was not by the laws of nature. The complete and utter randomness of where the earth happened to have been created and where it landed, in the perfect place in the universe for life to be, is that by coincidence?"

"What's to say it's not?" I asked.

"And I could say the exact same thing." Denny replied. "So where does consciousness come from? What we call a soul, huh?"

The last word was so childish I almost laughed. He was still so innocent. "I cannot say that I do or do not believe in an afterlife. It's not my decision to know what happens. But we were born in chemical conditions that caused life. Life under natural selection causes evolution and that those who were the best built for survival in what will become the human race had consciousness. If you haven't noticed, we are not the strongest, or best built, physically to live in the world. Consciousness causes us to live longer and then we can teach our children our consciousness and pass on beliefs that arose in that consciousness. People who do not conform, in history, have a tendency to be killed, and gods are invented to punish those who do not agree... we are at a place in history where we are free enough to know the truth."

"And the truth is that for the past couple hundred

thousand years of humanity… everyone has just been delusional?" he asked and put his head to one side.

"And it seems like every religion thinks other religions are all delusional too. That just sounds like it's not a very good system."

"I think that that says is for all of humanity there was always an understanding that beyond what we can see, and sense and so on that there is something that was uncreated, unconditional, something real that causes things to be as they are. And it also shows that humanity falls apart when left to itself."

"Oh yes, since we left God behind four hundred years ago we have fallen apart. We have sky rocketed forward!" I pressed.

"Just think about that statement. The very thing that you saw that made you lose your faith was a product of that loss of faith."

"Are you sure?" I asked. "Have I taught you nothing in history class? People have been brutally killing people since the very beginning of time. Real time and the time that you think exists in the Bible. Cain and Abel?"

"I don't believe that is anything more than a story." Denny sighed. "And I know that people have been killing each other for that long, but at the same time, to them, death was just death. It wasn't exactly the end of the world. It was the end of one world and the beginning of another. Now without faith people are terrified of death like it is the worst thing in the world."

"Everything you are talking about is the product of a different time and culture."

"You told me to read all those books. During the French revolution, people were practically lining up to be shot. In Ireland it was considered the best death to die as a martyr, to be killed, murdered for your beliefs. The Norse, they practically are begging to die in all that poetry. Are they all mad for expecting something else? Something after that?"

"Says you." I said. "Says the one that isn't dying."

"I'm just saying that it is clear that there never was a time when all people didn't believe something past them existing and it is clear that there was never a time when absolutely nothing existed, otherwise nothing would exist now. You cannot make nothing out of nothing."

"Denny it doesn't work that way."

"It doesn't work the other way either, Dr. Neal." he replied to me, his voice heated and stressed. "That's why it is called faith. There is no good explanation for either side of it, you just have to believe."

"Well, I don't." I replied. "I did once, then I tried, then I didn't, and then I tried again, and still didn't. So I'd rather be honest than a hypocrite." I took in a deep breath.

"But you still don't believe in miracles?"

"That would require something to do them and an infringement on the laws of nature!"

"Well, it seems pretty clear, of course only if you believed in something that was there to do it in the first place… that if that God made nature and thus the laws of nature, they could get around them."

"Wouldn't that be like God making a law and then changing his mind about that?"

"Not really, just getting around it to do something to

show power, usually." Denny tapped his finger on the edge of the plate.

"I teach, taught, classes on Early Christianity… and it looks like, in the Bible, God changed his mind, a lot. Noah?"

"I don't believe that actually happened…" Denny said.

"But it's in the book, so don't you have to believe it?" I stated.

"That's not how it works. We are at a point in history that we know that our ancestors did not exactly understand the reality of science and the world. Just because it is written in a way that could be understood as complete fact almost any other time in history, doesn't mean it doesn't hold any truth now. Besides, it is not like the book just magically appeared, in English, on someone's desk finished."

"Then how does it hold any validity?" I asked.

"I don't know! Alright? That is why it is called faith. I want to believe some of the words in that book."

"How can you take a part and not the whole?"

"You really need to take some theology courses…" Denny mumbled. "A lot of the Bible is actually just history. The book of Leviticus and many of the other books are in there even though we don't use it as law anymore. The reason it is there is so that we can see that the Hebrews were trying to be different than the rest of the world. They were keeping to a covenant they made, best they could, but they were still being human in the process. We don't take cues from the book of Joshua, in our faith, although the truth in that is that we are still fighting people we are scared of even though the New Testament just screams for us to accept differences. That last sentence has been ignored for a majority of the time in history, but that doesn't mean it was said without any backing to it." Denny was talking hurriedly, worried, shaking almost. "It just tells us how we should act, morally."

"I almost don't think morality exists…" I sighed. "It has changed by history, geography, economy and even a bonk in the head."

"So you don't think just walking into the middle of the street and killing someone is wrong?"

"What I think, doesn't matter. Other people, now and in history, have thought it perfectly acceptable. Those books I gave you, about the Danes, their form of morality is a far cry from anything the popular culture thinks today. To them it was completely acceptable to kill someone. In fact, it was an honorable thing to do, as long as they weren't your neighbor. In medieval England one of the biggest crimes was the rape of a virgin, now we don't even prosecute a good 15% of claims. They even managed to do better and castrated the men in the process." I laughed a bit. "Your morality is different than a man on Wall Street. So on and so forth. Besides, if such a thing as God existed, why would it need debating? Shouldn't it be obvious?"

Denny laughed and shook his head. "It didn't need debating till recently."

"That's because people were being killed if they thought differently and everything was run by it. It was like a corporation, not a faith."

"My point is, people who do have faith… we do see it,

right in front of us and just as we know we are breathing. It is obvious. We can see it, in a way. I don't know, people who don't believe are like blind to it or something, then they go into other explanations. Since like the Scientific Revolution… there was just nature, but then nature lost all rights as an entity and people just wanted to know, understand and then master nature. That was an obsession that just hasn't ended yet." He laughed and said, "They can't see the evidence. And what evidence we do have people treat God like he is a criminal. It is like the people are the police and they use all the evidence against God to convict him of something." Denny sighed and rubbed his hands together. "You believe in science, and I believe in both science and God, but either way we are both looking at something that was here long, long, long before us, and will exist long after we are gone… and it is independent of us but we are totally, and completely, dependent on it." He paused for a while and I didn't respond. "Just one thing that I do want to say, after all this, is that in my understanding, if God exists, then God is the most concrete thing there is, the most concrete thing there ever was." He leaned back and I didn't know what to say. I didn't believe, but I didn't go deaf to what he just said.

"When'd you become so smart?" I laughed.

His brow furrowed and a very small smile formed on his face. "That's what happens when you figure it out for yourself and don't just take what other people say for fact."

Chapter Twenty

I sat in my armchair, feeling like an angry ball of noodles. It was the oddest feeling; I had no control over anything in my body, that it was weak, but it obviously had a mind enough to tell me that it was angry. I was exhausted just breathing, and was choking most of the time when eating or drinking. I made the decision to go to hospice. Tess and I had looked at hospices when she was sick, she just never was put in one.

The decision was an odd one to make. It was literally the decision to die and to leave this house behind, the house I had been living in for over forty years as well my life, my job, career, and coworkers. Yet it was me accepting that I wasn't going to miraculously recover. There was no recovering from Parkinson's as far as I was aware. I hoped to God, wherever and whoever that was, if they existed at all that I wasn't going to waste away like my wife did. She didn't deserve that. I probably did, considering the things I did, but I could argue against it and be angry anyways.

I packed up some things, my radio, since I wanted to listen to it while I could. The hospice allowed pets, that was half the reason Tess and I looked at this one. I brought my favorite clothes, and the most comfortable and other things I thought I'd need. An employee of the hospice would drive me there. When they arrived, I looked back at the house and held the keys in my hand. My life was in there, covered in sticky notes, but it was in there. I had the house put on the market and things were getting moved around as soon as I left. I wasn't going to waste any time. I had my paperwork for the will and the house and everything else with me. I had specific paperwork for Denny in a manila envelope.

I was welcomed to the hospice by some very nice looking people. I knew it took special people to dedicate their lives to the dying. I received a suite-like rooming situation. There was a big comfortable bed with a TV in front of it, a place for my radio, a dresser, a bathroom and a small living room area. The employee, named Rose, helped me get situated and I sat in that bed and realized I was probably going to stay put right there for the rest of my life. They hooked me up to an IV and that made me feel like they deemed me incapable of drinking a glass of water. Well, I tried it recently and I couldn't. My hand would shake; the water would spill or the glass would drop. If I managed to get it to my face, it would go everywhere and then I'd choke on it if there was too much. A little was too much. That was my life. I had been drinking with straws and in small quantities, which is why they said I was very dehydrated and malnourished.

I turned the TV on; I wasn't much of a TV watcher but I was always trying new things these days. So I watched the news, learned about all the crap going on in the world from a very blonde, very ideal, young British woman talking calmly about a bombing like it didn't matter. Her voice only made a change of tone, in this case, interest, when there was a picture of a kitten shown and a story of said fluffy white kitten rescued from a drain.

I was annoyed by the stupidity and changed the channel. There were some old westerns on and it was interesting to hear such an odd old voice that used to be so prevalent on the TV. Voices changed much over time. It sounded like the people in my hometown growing up. It sounded so foreign and so old, but oddly welcoming as well.

There was a knock on the door. "Come in!" I said, my voice cracked and hissed, but I figured it sounded enough like the words I was trying to say. Denny opened the door and was carrying in a very cumbersome bag that he was struggling to hold onto. As soon as he shut the door behind him he put it down on the ground with a huff.

"What are you doing here?" I asked.

"I figured you must be bored out of your mind." he said. "You didn't tell me where you were going, so I asked Dr. Rogers." He put his bag down and pulled out a stack of books, but then a bottle of wine.

I laughed again and smiled, trying to sit up a bit further, but I had to press the button on the side of the bed to help me sit up. I still wore my good clothes. I had refused, and I mean refused, to wear those damn, stupid, cold, hospital gown things. He poured each of us a glass and I said, "I can't drink that, Denny."

"Why not?" he asked.

"Can't hold it. Just drink it yourself." I said.

"Alright." he sat down and was working on his homework on the couch. "I can drink for the both of us."

"You need to drive home, don't you?" I noted.

"Fine, just one glass then…" He paused for a while and pulled some things from his backpack. "You have to find an artist you like. I won't not rest until we found one. What about Giotto?" he asked. He held up a book. I recognized it immediately.

"He's an icon painter, nothing else. It's boring, too flat, no connection with any of the people in the images, non-realistic coloration. It's too early for any sophistication." I sighed. There was a look of disappointment on his face and he slumped just a little bit in the shoulders and put the book back into his bag.

"Well, I think it's amazingly sophisticated for the fourteenth century, Dr. Neal." Denny said matter-of-factly, and set the book aside. "Do you not like the Italians either?" he laughed and dug through this bag. "Botticelli?"

"He's much later and… less flat, Denny, but still just an icon painter. There is nothing more than Biblical figures, half of which are the Madonna and child. There are only so many versions of the same thing over and over again. Plus that poor woman in all the paintings looks down all the time, dejected looking and sad."

"That's because she knows that her kid is going to get brutally killed. Of course she isn't going to be all happy and stuff. But look at the delicacy and detail in these though is wonderful. The clothing has stiches and beautiful embroidery… there is a sense of place as well. Some of them even look like they belong in miniatures because of the bright color and compact detail, come on Dr. Neal, it's beautiful."

"You took too many art history classes. As beautiful as something is, it's not going to make me like it anymore unless I can make a connection to it. I have very little connection in this." I stated, sitting up the best I could in the bed. He took in a deep breath and put that back in his bag as well, which he swung onto the couch.

"Damn. Am I any closer?"

"Vermeer was the closest you got." I replied honestly.

"Well, speaking of art, I brought some!" He chuckled and pulled out some canvases from the very cumbersome bag. "They were made by Bridget."

"Why'd did you bring them?"

"I figured that you would rather stare at them than at the walls. It's pretty grey in here, Dr. Neal. These are cheery."

"When did you get the feeling I liked cheery things?" I asked.

"Everyone likes cheery things." he replied and he pulled them out and showed them to me. Some of them were nothing but color, smears of greens, blues and purples together, or bright, fiery colors. She seemed to have a thing for candles too, there were a lot of candles. Then there were a lot of birds, ones flying in the air, a few were too small to identify, some lovely woodpeckers, some eagles flying with fish caught in their talons. Most of them were quite simple, but if a young girl was fighting with hell inside her own body she might as well want to focus on the simplicity of the world around her. The last one Denny pulled out was of a ballerina, on one foot, the other one almost parallel with the rest of her. She was wearing white but there was an outline of a skull on her face and on her arms and her legs were bones. That poor girl, I thought, this was her. I knew well enough that this used to be her, and she couldn't dance anymore. She was in my place, she was just too weak, too frail. She'd probably break if she danced… or she'd end up killing herself. I supposed all she could do was paint it. Denny very calmly put the about ten paintings around the room. It really did make it a bit more colorful and cheerful. "I think I'll bring more soon. She's been very busy." He was hopping around a little in place. "So do you like them?"

"Yes, I appreciate the color. Tell your sister that they are very pretty."

He smiled and bounced even more. "I'm glad you like them Dr. Neal."

Chapter Twenty-One

I rested in bed, holding a book in front of me, although it was becoming difficult to do that much. I understood how little children felt when they tried to turn the pages. I needed those damned cardboard books, I might be able to handle them. There was a knock on the door. "Come in!" I said, the top of my voice being a raspy whisper. Bridget walked in.

"Hey Dr. Neal." she said, holding a paper bag on her hip.

"What are you doing here?" I asked.

"Interesting hello. Well the door isn't locked." she said and put the bag down. "I brought you some more paintings. I sealed them this morning."

"Thank you, they are very nice to look at." I replied, honestly. The color was truly welcomed. She began to set them out. She was wearing grey sweat pants probably made for a preteen and a spring weather coat that made shuffling noises as she set all the paintings out.

"I'm glad you like them. I wanted someone to see them."

"What do you think you'll do with them?" I asked,

trying to sit up a bit. I put the book aside, just next to me so I wouldn't have to reach later.

"I don't know. I haven't really thought about it… well I have but I haven't told anyone."

"And that would be?"

Her eyes looked upwards and then to the sides before they returned to me. "Denny would kill me if he knew…" She rubbed her hands together and sat down on the chair beside me. "I want people to have them once all of this is… uh… done. Like at the funeral and stuff."

"Is that why you're painting them?" I asked her.

She touched her hat a bit and adjusted it. "That's not why I started painting them, but that's why I'm making so many of them."

"So how'd you get here?"

She took off her coat and hung it behind her on the chair and held some car keys in her hand. "I drove." She paused for a moment and said, "I really just needed to get out of the house for a little while."

"Why?"

"Well, one, I've been stuck in there way too much, way too much… and then Denny was going a bit barmy when I left."

"You really do say that… what was he doing?" I asked and shook my head just a bit.

"He was panicking. It might be selfish of me to have left… I've acted like that plenty and Denny didn't go anywhere or do anything, but I couldn't see him like that. He broke like a vase on accident that I think used to be our grandmother's and he just started crying about like every-thing…"

"He's really stressed, Bridget." I stated. It was difficult for me to see Denny in any sort of non-rational state of mind. I had seen him drunk, but he didn't even act that oddly… but I was trying to imagine this kid who was almost always serene just losing it. I couldn't.

"He's been putting most of it on himself." Bridget said. "I know it's horrible and all, but he doesn't have to take on the responsibility he has."

"For both of us?" I added.

"Exactly. I'm glad he's your friend, Dr. Neal, and he doesn't seem to be all that stressed because of you… but he acts like I can't do anything myself. I am perfectly capable of doing a lot of things on my own and he doesn't seem to see that."

"Bridget, you are the only real family he has. You know that. He just wants to fix it. He thinks that he can, as many times as I have told him he can't. He will continue to act that way."

"Well why won't he listen to me when I tell him that I can do some things on my own?" she asked and crossed her arms. "I don't like this… this role reversal thing. I'm the older one. I used to be the one to help him tie his shoes, and put a tie on and look like he belonged at our school. I was the one that made sure he combed his hair and brushed his teeth and did his homework and went to class on time. He was always so distracted… and now…"

"He's doing all of that for you."

"Yes, and it just doesn't feel right…" She took in a deep breath. "I wish he'd just stop."

"I completely understand how he feels though." I affirmed. "My wife, she had pancreatic cancer. I acted just like he is now. I thought if I tried enough and cared enough it would go away; she'd be all better. I had to watch her decline. I had to dress her, bathe her, feed her, give her medicine."

"Shouldn't it be more stressful on me? I'm the one that's dying." Bridget stated strongly.

"You don't know that yet." I said.

"The doctors don't know that, but I do." Her eyes shook a bit just like her body did. They were a bit milky with a tint of yellow. They looked just like Tess's when she was sick. "I think a person knows when they aren't getting better and I'm not denying it."

"Denny can't understand how someone who is young like you could be sick. He understands that I'm old; this is normal. You are not a normal case."

She shook her head and looked around and took a heavy sigh. "It doesn't seem all that abnormal, really. I suppose I didn't get to do some of the stuff that other people get to do like having kids, getting married, having grandkids, a career… but I'm alright without that. I've spent my life raising my brother. Just knowing that he's going to go on to do so many wonderful things is good enough."

"Have you told him that?" I asked.

"No."

"He needs to hear it." I breathed. "Do you want to keep fighting?"

"What?"

"It's an important question that you need to deal with. Do you want to keep fighting or not? To get better."

"I know what I should say and why I should say it, but I really don't care. I'm going to keep going to treatment as horrible as it is, for Denny. I'm pretty damn finished with it at this point. But…"

"Then you're just done." I said. "This isn't something that you do for someone else, even your brother; this is your decision because it's your life."

She put her chin in her hand and sighed. "I don't think it's that easy, Dr. Neal. Henry… I mean Denny, he's literally my life. He doesn't want me to die."

"Do you have the option of living?" I asked. "Honestly."

"It's not much of an option, it's a chance. So, for him I'm going to take it. I'm not sure if I will ever be able to dance again if I do make it through, and I know that I'll never have children. I'm not sure what kind of future there will be for me, to be honest. All I want to do is dance, Dr. Neal. That's all… I don't know what else I can do. I wasn't smart like Denny. He absorbed everything around him. I couldn't look at books because I couldn't understand it like he did' I couldn't take in the information and process it. But with dancing, I could understand everything, I felt free and something more than human. I always imagined humans as trapped in the confines of their body, and now I feel that, but for a few years I felt like I was free from all of that. I suppose in a way it is selfish of me to want to stay longer, although I say it's for Henry, he's the one that has to take care of me." She bit her lip just like Denny did when he was nervous. "So, I don't really know." Her eyes flashed to me. "You've taken care of a dying person, what do you think?"

"What do I think?" I repeated. I took in a deep breath and looked at my glass of water. I reached for it but stopped. She stood up and handed it to me, although she was holding it as I took some sips. I just pretended like I could do it myself. "Thank you." I paused. "I honestly think it is worse to be a caregiver than the dying person. As I said, Denny just wants to make it all better. When my wife was sick, that's what I kept thinking. I was running myself into the ground with exhaustion and worry and stress and anger that it wasn't doing anyone any good. I was getting short with myself, but never with Tess…"

Her eyes lit up again. "Denny is just like that. When I have bad days, he becomes the calmest person I've ever seen, very diligent and completely disconnected… but like today, when I have good days, he just let's all of it out. He can't help that he's feeling that way but he only releases it when it's a… I wouldn't say good, but a better time."

"I did that a lot. It was odd to see a woman who carried my son, given birth to him and buried him, the strongest woman I had ever known, to be so small that I could carry her… and so weak that I had to clean her and feed her until she died. It was odd. I disconnected a lot. If I didn't, I probably wouldn't be able to handle it."

"I don't want to get to that point…" Bridget mumbled and looked around. "Henry already had to do those things for me. I was so out of it then, but I knew that it happened… and I'm still embarrassed that my little brother had to help me bathe, had to feed me, had to clean me up because I couldn't do it myself. But I don't want that to be normal…"

"Well honey, I'm already there." I said. "But I wouldn't say I'm used to it either." She pulled her hat off and crunched the knitted yarn in her hands. Her head was very shiny. "You should go without the hat more often." I said.

"Really? You don't think it looks weird?"

"I mean your head might get cold, but it's not weird at all."

"Ella made me this hat. She likes to knit."

I smiled and said, "I've noticed. Denny has a hat that she made. Have you reconnected with her at all?"

She nodded and said, "I was mad at them both for a little while because they didn't tell me they were dating, but it's no use being mad at anyone really. I'm happy that Henry has someone, and Ella is a great person. She was one of my best friends, and I guess in a way she still is. Henry needs her in his life." She looked around the room at her own paintings. "That's a lot of birds…" she mumbled.

"It is." I breathed. "I like birds."

"I wish I could fly again." she said.

"I thought so. I can tell in your paintings, there's a lot of birds in this room."

"A lot of birds live outside our patio. There's a tree that they live in and I can just paint them all the time because there are so many kinds. I tried paintings squirrels and cats and stuff but I didn't like that…" She stood up and helped me get another drink from my glass. She sat and stared ahead for a moment and said, "Have you had dreams where you're dead, Dr. Neal?"

"What do you mean?" I asked.

"Or it's like you are. I've had a dream where I was just walking around in nothing. There was absolutely nothing but black. I couldn't hear anything or see anything or feel anything. It was like I was just nowhere and it was terrifying. I was walking towards something though, trying to find a way out or light or I don't even know…" She sat cross legged now and put her hands on her knees. "But then I've had dreams where I was sitting on the shore, watching the sunset, and everything was perfect. The air was the right temperature, the wind was refreshing, the waves were lapping up against my feet and the water was clear. It was peaceful, but I knew I wasn't alive. I could hear birds, lots of birds and behind me was a forest, but it wasn't scary like I would get lost in it, but inviting. But I stayed by the shore, where there was a boat. The boat was grey and attached to a little pole by a thin rope. I ended up getting in the boat and coming back. I don't know why I made that decision in the dream, that's just how it happened."

"I haven't had dreams like that." I said. "I don't dream a lot."

"About anything?" Her head cocked to one side in curiosity.

"I've had dreams, but they were different in a way. I've dreamed about being back in Vietnam. I've had dreams where my wife was alive again, and where my son was alive again, but that's about it."

"Have you had dreams about flying?" she asked. I shook

my head no. "They're really wicked. It's like you are just running and then you are flung off the ground and into the air and for a moment you think it's the coolest thing ever. Then you know that you are going to have to hit the ground again and it's scary. People usually wake up right before they hit the ground, but I always hit the ground. And it hurts. Then it happens all over again, but the second time it's not fun at all. It's like trying to run away from something that's pulling on strings attached to you, getting you into the air and having you crash and burn... it's horrible."

"I thought you said you wanted to fly." I asked and pulled on the blanket that was on my legs. I was shivering from the cold. She stood up and picked up an afghan that was on my feet and put it around my shoulders. She acted like what she was doing was so simple and then she sat right back down.

"It really isn't flying. There isn't any control in it. I don't make the decision to go up into the air and I'm not in the air for a long enough period of time for it to count really, although it feels like ages." She rubbed her hands together and her phone began to ring. "Shit, it's Hen... Denny."

She answered it and I could hear his voice on the other end. "Damn, calm down, I'm fine, I'm fine." She rubbed her forehead now and took in a deep breath. "I'm visiting Dr. Neal. What? Henry calm down, really, this isn't necessary. Henry? Henry!" She looked at her phone and said, "He hung up. He's probably coming over here." She buried her head in her hands and took in a deep breath and then coughed. She was nervously rubbing her leg although the look on her face implied pain. She looked at me and said, "So I can tell someone before he comes, the last doctor's appointment I went to I didn't let Henry come into the room just because and they said I have a 14% chance of recovering. It spread, and I know that you said something to him about it being preventable and all... and I beat myself up over it a lot. I wasn't careful in the first place and then didn't get to the doctor until it was quite late in the game because I guess when you are young you... feel like you're invincible."

"I didn't mean anything offensive by what I said to Denny." I said.

"Just the truth unfortunately... if I just did something when I felt shitty the first time maybe it wouldn't have gotten so far. I just didn't want anyone to know..." she muttered.

"Is he coming over here?" I asked.

"Yes... sorry, I didn't come to cause stress... but I don't know how he's going to act..." she was continuing to bite her lip and rubbing her left leg.

We both fell quiet until he came. His hair was a mess; his face was utterly blank but there was distress in his eyes. "Bridget, why did you leave the house without me?"

"Henry, I can drive. I'm perfectly capable. I wasn't going to stay there and listen to you yelling." She crossed her arms and looked straight ahead, past me.

"Come on Bridget, you need to get home."

"I don't want to go home."

"Come on Bridget." he pressed.

"Denny, if she doesn't want to go she doesn't have to." I said calmly.

His eyes flashed at me, in anger. "How do you know what's best for her? She missed her medicine and she could have gotten killed on the way here!"

"I didn't miss my medicine..." Bridget muttered. "I took it, I swear."

"Then you didn't take it on time! You know what the"

"Yes, yes, I know what the doctor's say, now calm down Henry! Damn it." Bridget's brow furrowed and Denny paced a bit, taking in breath quickly, putting his hands up to his mouth.

"Bridget, we need to go home. Sorry for the intrusion Dr. Neal." he said. His voice was quiet. I could hardly hear it.

"Hold on, hold on. Neither of you actually want to go back to that house." I stated. "Bridget left for a reason, and obviously that house is just making you stressed out. Go somewhere else." I used as much force as I could manage behind my voice and it still sounded like a simple request filled with wispy air. "Denny?" I said again and he looked at me and then to his sister.

"Where would you like to go?" he asked.

"Can we go see a film?" she replied. "We haven't done that in a while. I could go for some popcorn." Her voice was calm, happy, and relaxed... she could get over Denny's tirade quickly.

"Sure, sure, we can do that." He looked over to me and said, "I don't like that you are stuck here all day either."

"It's fine..." I muttered. It was a lie. I hated this room

and I hated being in it but I didn't exactly have another choice.

Bridget said, "We could watch the film here. I'm sure they have popcorn around here somewhere and there's a microwave." She looked over to me with a kind, smiling face. "That way you can see it too."

"I don't have any here." I sighed. "Films."

Denny sighed, "I'll have to go back to the house to get Bridget's meds anyways, I can pick up some popcorn and a film on my way back." He stood with an arm around his stomach and one hand on his shoulder, rubbing the facial hair he had on his cheeks. It was annoying me.

"While you're there, either shave all of it, or just make it into something, the whole sporadic hair thing is annoying me." I said. "I don't think I could see it all night."

There's that smile. There it is. He nodded and said, "Shall do, Dr. Neal. Shall do."

After he returned, Bridget left to go find the restroom. Denny took in a deep breath and looked at me. I said to him, "You need to lighten up buddy."

I'm not exactly how that elicited the response that came though, because his eyes just began to burn and he cried, "Lighten up? You want me to lighten up? Yes, because I can just turn on a switch and all this bloody shit can just go away as if it never even happened! I can't just lighten up!" he hissed, the last sentence and seemed to shrink into himself.

"Just act like it, for your sister."

"I act like it all the time! I act like everything's alright when it's not! So, I broke? What does it matter? I can't just keep acting…"

"Well, you kind of chose it as your career choice, so at least it's good practice." I said.

"Why do you not take anything seriously? Really? I don't understand!"

"Me, not taking anything seriously? You must be seriously joking because that is the oddest statement I've ever heard!" I looked at him and felt the heat rushing towards my face. His hand grasped the chair. He looked like he was about to speak. "Don't even think about saying that I don't understand, because I understand; I understand everything. I know what you are thinking, feeling; I know all of it but you cannot even think about understanding me for a moment." Bridget came back in and we fell silent.

Before Denny left I said, "Just go out and get drunk tonight. It might actually help."

Chapter Twenty-Two

Denny came most days, and would sit on the couch and do his homework and ask me questions about his paper. He was doing well, he just got distracted easily. Whenever Racer wanted attention, the dog would come before his paper. He was always on his phone talking to his girlfriend. He brought more paintings. There were beautiful blue birds sitting in the branches of trees, their red bellies bright against the background. There were some black birds, mid-flight, just their bodies with a white background. She paid amazing attention to their feathers. I was getting to know this young woman more than I ever thought I would. I could see her thought processes. She was such a positive girl, or at least she was desperately trying to be. There was such brightness in these works, but it was obvious that all she wanted to do was fly and get away from herself. She saw herself as the ground-bound skeleton that she showed me earlier. She was ready to go, just as I was. I was only hoping that she didn't have to go right now. I was hoping that she'd get better. I didn't know if that cheerfulness she showed was hope to go on, or the hope that it would be over soon.

Denny approached me with a big smile across face. "Alright, I think I found something, give it a chance, ignore the man's name."

"What is it?" I asked. My voice was little more than a whisper now. He didn't respond. "You mentioned it."

"Courbet."

"French…"

"Uh huh, ignore that. Just look purely at the art." It was from the mid-eighteen hundreds. The art was smoky, shadowy, but there was eye contact with most of it, although as Denny flipped through the pages there was a lot of self-portraits and a lot of naked women that weren't what I would consider anatomically correct. The people were otherwise realistic although there was an enormous amount of landscapes and I didn't like the landscapes. They were cold and unrealistic. Only the figures in them, if there were figures, seemed to hold any life. There were many dead and dying deer in his paintings, all being hunted in some manner, and yet I felt the most connected to those. The ones dying had such a pain and worry in their eyes. I didn't want to look like that. I did, though. I looked like that.

"You're closer but not there yet…"

"Aw… almost there?" I nodded a bit and closed my eyes for a brief moment. "Well, I'll get there, don't worry."

"I'm not worrying…" I said. I didn't know what this desperation was he held for wanting me to truly love some kind of art he appreciated. We were different people, that had already been well established. Yet he was going to keep trying. Stubborn young man. Stubbornness was always a good quality.

I got weaker by the hour, though. I could feel it. By the time Denny managed to come up with another artist, I could barely speak. Denny would take Racer on walks and play with him outside. I tried really hard to talk, but after two weeks, I was just blinking to speak or to make my opinions known. One blink meant no, two meant yes, so on and so forth. That was how I helped Denny do his homework. If he had questions, they had to be yes or no. I was otherwise useless. He had Google to ask.

So, when he came forward and opened the last art book I was very impressed. Rembrandt. It had smoky, deliberate strokes, beautiful color, good eye contact, amazing detail, attention to the historical context of the biblical figures, as much as possible. The way light was used was perfect, and I felt like this was it. I blinked a lot just to let him know. "Did I find it? Did I do good?" I blinked twice. Well, Denny, the word is well. He smiled and jumped up and down. He began to close the book. I blinked once. "You want to see more of it? Alright, alright." He then looked around and said, "I have something else I have to show you…" He pulled his bag near to him and wrapped his arms around it. "So. remember what we talked about while we were cleaning out your storage room? I thought about it." He rubbed the back of his head. "I'm not sure what I'm going to do… and I know that my reasoning behind it is not good but…" He pulled out a ring box and opened it. "I'm going to ask Ella at some point… I want my sister to be involved as long as she can and this would make her really happy." Damn it boy, this is supposed to make you happy and this girl of yours is happy, I thought. I didn't exactly include money in that envelope for a wedding. I hoped that his parents would get that stick out of their asses and actually help their son with this. It's not like they haven't hawked up money for them to go to that fancy school, they should be able to pay for this.

"Do you like it? I didn't exactly have money for it, so I put it on a payment plan. Apparently, people do that a lot less often than I thought they did. I had to convince the jeweler people to let me do that." He spoke so quickly and excitedly I could barely keep up. "But it looks so cool! I didn't know I had any artistic talent in me. I thought that all went to my sister, but this is pretty fine." He opened it again and put it near me for a moment before carefully placing it back in his bag. That boy... really? "I know you really don't know Ella that much, except for the history of her name... which I must say that wasn't the best thing in the world to tell her..." Well no duh kid, that's why I did it. I wanted to see if she could handle weird conversation. It made her lose her appetite though, which was pretty funny... although she really needed to eat more anyways. "But I've been with her for about two years, which isn't a lot these days I know... but those two years have been the most stressful, crazy times of my life, so if she could handle me then, and I could handle her then too, then we should be able to make it work. And I really thought about what you said. The reason I made this decision is that I tried to picture my life without her in it, whether or not someone else was involved, and I couldn't."

That's good, that's good. I really wished that I could hug him. I really wished that I could tell him how proud I was of him and that he was going to be a great person. He already was. "But I don't know how I'm going to ask her! Ahhh.... I have to figure that out." He stood up from where he had sat on the side of my bed and began to pace. He was blurring the color behind him. The paintings by now had covered almost every surface of this room.

"What if I take her to dinner and I put the ring on a breadstick and she goes to eat one of the breadsticks and the ring is on the breadstick!" He looked at me pointing a finger. I blinked once. "No? Moonlight walk on the beach?" No. "Too cliché? Yeah, but it's better than the breadstick option I suppose... what if I get a big cake and put it on the cake?" Why does he keep wanting to put something that cost more than his rent inside food? No. "Yeah, I'd end up eating most of the cake, which is fine. I don't know how she lives on the diet she is on. I mean she could probably eat three times more and nothing would happen, but she's not convinced of that. Oh, I know! I know! She has a perform-ance coming up! I could talk to the people who are with her. I know the guy she dances with, I can't pronounce his name, he's from... Austria I think." I blinked a few times and half laughed. "Oh no, he's not competition don't worry. But what if for like their last scene or something I go out there. Could you imagine how freaking confused she'd be!" He was laughing and jumping up and down just slightly. Wearing those horrible costumes? "Is it a good idea?" I wasn't sure. People pay to go see those things, if he ruins it... "Dr. Neal!" I blinked one and a half times. "What does that mean?" What was I going to say? I couldn't say anything! "Work on it?" Blinked twice.

"Well what if I just do it at their dress rehearsal... oh no that's in like three weeks away! I need to call what's-his-face!"

Chapter Twenty-Three

I was fast asleep. I wasn't sure what I was dreaming about. I couldn't hardly think anymore some days. My mind would wander away and then come back and I'd be dazed and confused, but I didn't lose that much time. It wasn't like I was missing anything either. The nurses would come in and try turning on the TV, but I was still able to make grunts. I would stand it for about an hour at a time, or one program at a time, but I hated the crime shows that were always on. Daytime TV didn't seem like it was worth anything. Documentaries were occasionally interesting, though, and sometimes I could watch a few of them before falling off to sleep.

I heard the door open. My eyes blinked and my vision was temporarily blurry. I just saw a man wearing white. He was massive, muscular, with oddly blonde hair. I blinked some more wondering if I was crazy. My heart beat a bit faster because I couldn't recognize the guy and couldn't see him very clearly. Finally, I could see. Was I dead? No, no, Denny was standing right next to him. I'm alive, I told myself. But who the hell was this massive man? He stood properly, his hands together in front of him, he looked like Captain America to be completely honest, until he spoke and he sounded German. Ah, it's the Austrian guy… what's his face.

"Hello, I'm Helmut. I'm a friend of Henry's."

Denny sighed and smiled. "This is Ella's dance partner. I told you about him. He helped me decide what to do when I propose. So, it looks like for the last scene, Ella will be up at the front of the stage and normally he'd come up behind her, mirror what she does and then they walk off stage together at the end. Helmut here," He looked to the man. "Did I pronounce your name right?"

"Good enough."

"Well, he said that I could be with the other performers who are in the background sitting. Instead of him going up and dancing with Ella, I could go up there and there is a point when we'd face and then I could propose."

Helmut started to clap his hands and jump up and down just a bit and it was hilarious. Oh my God, this man… oh my God… if I could laugh then I would. "You know, Henry, when you take my place and come behind her, she'll know that it's not me. You're a little man. You carry yourself differently, you walk differently, and you don't know how to dance. She'll know. She'll probably become uncomfortable and confused. So, when she turns to face you, she might be a bit angry. She's really a perfectionist. She doesn't like when things go wrong." His accent wasn't that bad really, very easy and understandable.

"Dr. Neal," Denny looked over to me. "We needed a place to practice. We couldn't do it at my house because then Bridget would find out and then it wouldn't be a surprise. We were going to do it at Helmut's apartment, but he lives with five other people from the school, and then they'd know. It's supposed to be a secret, and we really can't practice at the school. But this way you can know what we are doing and no one else will know." Since when did he think this was a good idea? Well, I thought, I wasn't going to be bored for a while.

Helmut began, "First you need to learn to walk."

"I know how to walk."

"No, no, no, you need to learn to walk like a dancer. Alright? Watch me." Helmut stood up, his shoulders back and he stepped forward very gingerly foot by foot, each foot pointed and then occasionally he'd do a skipping like motion. "Did you see?"

"Yes…" Denny sighed. "I'm going to look like a fool."

"You're going to look like a fool if you walk normally on stage surrounded by classically trained dancers. Try." Denny nodded and stepped forward. After one step Helmut shook his head. "No, no, no," He put his hands on Denny's shoulders and pulled them back. "Don't slouch. Stand up more than straight, a curve in your spine. Point your toes, stretch out your legs. Hands behind your back." Denny's eyes bugged out and he tried again. "Better, better, but slower. Be deliberate Henry. People are going to know if you aren't part of the group if you don't at least pretend like you know what you are doing."

"Well, I haven't exactly been doing this for years like the rest of you…"

"All you have to do is walk right now. Focus on that."

Denny kept walking back and forth until Helmut thought it was acceptable. "There you are. See? You can do it."

"One problem, I'm not a graceful person."

"And Ella is quite aware of that." Helmut crossed his massive arms and laughed. "I hear about you all the time."

"You should see her when she's ice skating. She falls all over the place."

"I was the one that took her to the rink to practice so she wouldn't."

"She did practice, I knew it!"

"I didn't particularly want to hear about it when she fell all over the place again in front of you."

"Because you have to put up with her criticism all the time."

"And you don't?" Helmut asked laughing. "I'm sure she discusses your wardrobe plenty." He paused and said, "And speaking of which, so you fit in… you'll be wearing a costume."

"You must be joking." Denny blinked quickly and took in a deep breath. "I… I thought I could just wear a nice suit or sweater or something."

"No, no, no, if you are dancing with us, you need to fit in. I already talked to the lady who works in the costume shop. You're about the size of someone I work with and I talked to him, he has a costume that you can borrow."

"I don't have to wear tights, do I?"

"They're not that bad." Helmut replied.

"I'm not wearing tights. No, no, no."

He crossed his arms again. "You've worn tights before though."

"Plenty of times, but I'm sure as hell not going to when I'm asking my girlfriend to marry me." Denny replied.

"Well, I will see what I can do." Helmut said. "Alright the next part of the dance. You will come up behind her. She will not be looking at you, you are just mirroring her movements, but in a more masculine fashion."

"I'm not sure how to be masculine while wearing tights…"

"You might not have to be wearing tights, and they were originally made for men." Helmut said. "Alright, what she will be doing is this." He stretched out his arms and began to walk across my floor and jumping up in the air, his legs parallel to the ground.

"I can't do that." Denny replied. "I won't be able to do that."

"I'm quite aware that you won't be able to do that. But I'm letting you know that is what she will be doing. I'm supposed to do that, but you will just walk behind her with your arms out parallel to hers and just walk like I showed you. Do a little skip like I showed you earlier so your feet are off the ground when her legs are off the ground." Denny nodded and they tried that a few times. "Then when you get to stage left then she will stop. Make sure you are still behind her. She'll be facing the audience and you need to be right behind her. Whatever she does, just make sure you are behind her doing something similar. Alright? That's really all you need to remember. Then she'll suddenly turn around and face you. That's when you propose. Alright?"

"Alright." Denny said.

"And Henry, there are no words. Don't speak. Just get down on your knee and open up the box and let that speak for you. She won't speak either, I'm sure. She'll probably act like it's all part of the performance. She has this thing that during the whole ballet, even when she's not on the stage, she won't speak. Alright?"

"Yep." Denny took in a breath. "I can't talk?"

"That's what I said." Helmut said. "Please no speeches."

"But I've been like making speeches in my head…"

"You can use them afterwards." Helmut said. "Especially if she says no, then you can use it later to convince her."

His eyes bugged out, and he put an arm around his middle and up to his shoulder. He was nervous. "I… I hope she says yes. I wasn't really planning anything else."

"Of course, you weren't." Helmut said. "She'll say yes, I'm sure. She talks about you enough."

"What does she say?" Denny asked.

"Well, she normally lets me know when you've had dates, where you had the date…" He laughed and said, "She let me know about the first time you stayed over, don't worry it wasn't bad, what she said. I'm like her therapist."

"Well, that's interesting because she's mine." Denny then rubbed his hands together and said, "Well, I'd like to apologize for the last few years of issues I've caused."

"Oh, don't worry. You haven't caused issues. She's no more stressed than she was before you came along. Well, she is, but that's because she's getting into more intense work… and she's a principle now, which is her first time. So that's more stress, but you know that, and it's not because of you." Helmut stood back and said, "Alright, once more. Let's see how you do. It might actually be easier when you are on stage because she'll be there, if the nerves don't get to you first, but I'd assume you'd be fine since you're an actor and all."

Denny nodded and proceeded to waltz across the living area then put his arms up and he looked hilarious. He looked so awkward and out of place. "Do something with your face." Helmut said. "That expression isn't going to work." Denny was facing away now and I couldn't see what he was doing. "Don't smile like that. Don't hardly smile. Just look confident. That's all you have to do." Helmut put his hands on his face and his hands slid down and he took in a deep breath. "Close enough, close enough. You'll only be up there for like five minutes at maximum." Helmut patted his back with enough force that I thought the poor boy would be knocked to the ground. He braced himself and took in a deep breath. "Now we have something else that needs to be dealt with. Your wardrobe. Just so I don't have to listen to Ella complain about it after two get married... we need to go through your current wardrobe and go shopping."

"I can't afford new clothes."

"Then it will be an engagement present, but I'm doing this for my own sanity. Before you go on that stage you better wash your hair, blow dry it, brush it, and make sure that it doesn't look like that mess that you normally walk around with." Denny put his hand on his head and touched it nervously.

"You people keep making me want to wear hats, all the time." He looked over to me. "He made me cut my hair."

"Thank you!" Helmut exclaimed. "I'm not sure Ella would have been able to handle the mess."

"Thanks. My sister thought it was adorable."

Helmut shook his head and crossed his arms. "You are old enough that you need to be professional. Adorable is not a word you want to be classified as." Thank you! Thank you! Well at least there is someone who will keep him looking acceptable around here.

"People call you adorable all the time."

"Yes, the way I act, not the way I look. Does this look adorable to you?" He stretched out his arms.

"Looks kind of intimidating to me to be completely honest."

"Exactly." He put his arms down to the side.

"Well I have been working out lately."

"Really?" he went and poked Denny in the side and Denny scrunched over.

"What was that for?"

"Working out?" Helmut asked, laughing.

"Yeah." Helmut poked him in the stomach then. "What the hell?"

"Hit me in the stomach." Helmut said.

"What?"

"You heard me."

"I'm not doing that." Denny replied.

"Henry, just do it."

"Fine, fine." So he went to punch the man in the stomach but nothing happened when Denny's fist made contact. His hand just stopped.

"That's working out." Helmut said staunchly.

"You didn't feel that?"

"Well I know you did it but it didn't hurt." Helmut replied.

"Not all of us can be dancers."

"Never thought that being a ballerina could be so manly." Helmut smiled cheekily. He put his hands on his hips and stood to the side.

Chapter Twenty-Four

When it got too quiet, Denny would start thinking out loud. I was always falling asleep, which was embarrassing for me, but that was alright. He chose to be here, to give me some company. He always kept me up to date about his sister. She wasn't getting any better or worse. He was still hopeful for her. I only wanted everything to go well for both of them.

I got to the point that I knew I was almost there. I could smell my own death. I could feel that I wasn't going to live much longer. I was becoming worried, and curious, but at times I was just too tired to give a shit. I just wanted to be done with all this, to just close my eyes and them not open again. It seemed so simple in that respect. Yet everyone seemed to believe that something was going to happen after that, and that was the part that was giving me grief. I didn't know what was going to happen. I didn't know if I actually wanted to be a ghost or not as that was the only theory that I had held onto and it was mostly a joke. All I knew was that I wanted to see my wife, son and my parents, all of my friends. It was exhausting questioning and wondering. The curiosity was painful.

All but one friend though. Denny was still going to be here, and he was still going to be chiseling away, hammering out a life for himself and he needed help with that. I wasn't going to be here in person to help guide him along but I had something else for him.

I had to get him to come over to my bedside. I tried moving my hands, but that didn't work. So, I just breathed really loudly. He looked over at me and I was blinking like a maniac. "Yes?" He smiled and walked over. My bag with the letter to Denny was on the table. I moved my eyes so they looked at the table. "This over here?" he asked. I blinked twice. "Do you want me to bring it over to you?" I blinked twice again. He opened it up and said, "Do you want the folder?" Twice. "Do you want me to open it?" Twice again. He opened it and there was a big envelope that said, "Henry Helling" on it.

I needed to say something. So, I mustered up all my strength, and focused, "No surrender." That was all I could manage to say.

"Je ne parle pas la langue de rachat." he replied. I blinked once, signaling that I didn't understand. "I don't speak surrender language."

Dear Denny,

Enclosed is a check. This should manage to cover your living expenses throughout your graduate school as well as your sister's medical expenses. I also wish for you to have my dog, Racer. He could be very helpful to Bridget as well. You will be given the wine left in the cellar of my house, as I figure that you will need it. I wish to thank you for the kindness you have shown me. I do not know if you understand how much it means to an old man to have a friend. Thank you.

Neal.

My body felt oddly clammy. I hadn't really been able to move in weeks and it was annoying. It was an adventure to take in a deep breath. There was intense feeling that I had to breathe, and that was to be expected, but it took a lot of effort. I simply focused on just breathing when I fell asleep. I was beginning to hate sleep. It was too close to death in many ways, but it wasn't the real thing. I wasn't sure why I hated it so much, whether I was scared I wasn't going to wake up or because I would. Common sense would state that I hoped for. It was the worst kind of prison possible. I was stuck in my own body, unable to move, unable to take in reasonable breath, unable to fill my hungry stomach or my thirst, or to scratch an itch. I wasn't able to get around in one of those fancy wheelchairs, I was just stuck in a bed. My mind was working just fine though. I was aware of everything, although I was old enough that I'd randomly drift off to sleep and back.

And there I was, sleeping soundly. For once, I actually had a dream. I felt like I was where Bridget said she had dreams about, a shore. It was a rocky shore with beige plants springing up from in between the rocks. Yet it was easy to sit upon the rocks near the water. The water was warm, almost as if it didn't have a temperature different from my body. The wind smelled sweet and came from behind me. I stood up. I could walk again, perfectly able and comfortable with my own body. I felt almost strong again. I loved it. As I walked I could feel all the pebbles on my bare feet. I heard a bark and looked toward the forest. I saw Titan running towards me. He was smiling and energetic. He ran up and stopped right before me. I leaned over and pet him and then lay on the ground while he licked my face. "There you are boy. You are doing real well here, aren't you?" I looked back to the forest. I was hoping to see my wife come after him, or my son. Yet no one followed him. It was just this old dog that suddenly acted like a puppy again. He rushed into the water and right back out, shaking off the excess happily. I stood up and continued to walk along the water, occasionally into it.

I could hear a loud noise, but couldn't tell where it was from. "Dr. Neal. Dr. Neal?"

I opened my eyes. I was back in the hospice and angry that I was. I couldn't see immediately. "Dr. Neal?" There was another voice, a woman's voice. I didn't completely recognize it. I took in a deep breath, using all the energy I could. Denny and Ella were standing to my right. Denny's arm was around her and they were both smiling. She looked like she had just come from a performance. Her hair was in a perfect hazel bun in the back of her hair, not one hair was out of place. There was makeup on her face that no one would normally wear in public. Denny's hair looked nice. "Dr. Neal?" Denny began. "Hi, I just wanted to let you know she said yes."

Nina Wilson

About the Author

Nina Wilson is a graduate of Coe College in Cedar Rapids Iowa. She lives in Indianola Iowa with her family. She loves history, especially early English history, photography, traveling, fishing, and camping.